RUGBY
WARRIOR

GERARD SIGGINS was born in Dublin and has lived almost all his life in the shadow of Lansdowne Road; he's been attending rugby matches there since he was small enough for his dad to lift him over the turnstiles. He is a sports journalist and worked for the *Sunday Tribune* for many years. His first book about rugby player, Eoin Madden, *Rugby Spirit*, is also published by The O'Brien Press.

RUGBY WARRIOR

GERARD SIGGINS

THE O'BRIEN PRESS
DUBLIN

First published 2014 by
The O'Brien Press Ltd,
12 Terenure Road East, Rathgar,
Dublin 6, D06 HD27, Ireland.
Tel: +353 1 4923333; Fax: +353 1 4922777
E-mail: books@obrien.ie.
Website: www.obrien.ie
Reprinted 2014, 2015.
ISBN: 978-1-84717-591-5
Text © copyright Gerard Siggins 2014
Copyright for typesetting, layout, editing, design
© The O'Brien Press Ltd

8 7 6 5 4 3
18 17 16 15

Printed and bound by CPI Group (UK) Ltd, Croydon, CR0 4YY
The paper in this book is produced using pulp from managed forests

The O'Brien Press receives financial assistance from

DEDICATION

To my brothers Aidan and Ed, and sister Ethel

ACKNOWLEDGEMENTS

Thank you to all at The O'Brien Press for their encouragement, especially my long-suffering editor, Helen Carr. Thanks to my family and friends for their support, and various U13 rugby, cricket and soccer teams for providing inspiration – you know who you are. And thanks to the many schools, bookshops and libraries that have given me the opportunity to talk to readers about Eoin, Brian and the world of school sport.

CHAPTER 1

'**M**ind the cow pats, Eoin!' came the call from behind the goalposts. 'Ah … too late …' the voice called again.

Eoin Madden looked up and grinned. He had been kicking a ball over the crossbar for half an hour, but hadn't seen his grandfather, Dixie Madden, arrive. He rambled over to where the old man was leaning on the rail that surrounded the Ormondstown Gaels GAA pitch.

'You're kicking well,' said Dixie, 'but it's cheating to use those Gaelic posts – they're a good bit lower, aren't they?'

'Yeah, I suppose so,' said Eoin, picking the rugby ball up carefully from where it sat atop a crusty slab of cow manure. 'The crossbar is two and a half metres high, and in rugby it's three metres. The GAA goal is a good bit wider too, but sure it's good practice and it's quiet here today.'

'Your mother tells me you're getting ready to get back up to Castlerock next week?'

'I suppose I am,' replied Eoin. 'I had a great summer and the Gaels had a good run in the championship too, but I really missed the rugby, to be honest. I must be the only thirteen-year-old in the country who can't wait for the holidays to end and to get back to school!'

'Well, you look like you're getting back in the groove,' grinned Dixie. 'That last kick was as good as the one you made to win the Father Geoghegan Cup.'

'That was a great day, wasn't it?' Eoin replied, with a smile. 'I'd love to play in the Aviva again someday.'

'I must say, that whole day was a huge tonic,' said Dixie. 'I was treated like royalty and then to cap it all you really showed some class to keep your nerve for the kick. I was just looking at the scrapbook last night, because Andy Finn sent me on some great photos of the game I'll have to put into it. Maybe you'll give me a hand with that tonight?' he asked.

'I'd like that,' said Eoin, 'but I've set myself a target of a hundred kicks this afternoon and I have a few more to go, so I'd better get back to work now if that's OK?'

Dixie laughed and waved him back to his mark. 'That's some dedication, Eoin; mind you don't wear down the toe of that boot before the season starts!' before he wandered away towards his car.

Eoin teed up the ball a bit further away on the right, and gave himself a more difficult angle, but still split the posts. 'Huh, smaller target my eye,' he muttered to himself, 'I'd put them over even if it was half the width!'

He carried on with his practice for another ten minutes before he was interrupted again. This time it was a new Ormondstown Gaels team-mate called Dylan.

'Howya, Eoin,' chirped Dylan, who was about a foot smaller than Eoin and wore his hair shorter than a tennis ball.

'I'm grand, Dylan, what's going on with you?'

'I've a bit of news actually. I'm off to Dublin next week – they're sending me to Castlerock. Isn't that where you go?'

'It is indeed, that's great news. It'll be good to have another bogger to share the loudmouth Leinster fans with!'

Dylan looked a bit nervous. 'I'm not sure about that, I'm Leinster myself – Drogheda – don't they teach you Geography up in Castlerock? Leinster's not just about Blackrock and Dublin 4 you know. So, if you're getting grief for being a Munster fan then you're still on your own,' he grinned.

'Ha, thanks a bunch, pal! Are you any use at the rugby? It's pretty big up there in Castlerock.'

'Yeah, we lived in Limerick for a while too, so I picked it up. I wasn't bad at scrum-half they told me.'

'Well I didn't have you marked out as a second row, anyway, unless they've started a Smurfs rugby team …' laughed Eoin, as he skipped out of the way of Dylan's lame attempt to throw a punch. 'I'll see you before you go, and give you the lowdown on what to expect. But I've got to dash, just remembered Mam told me to be home early. It's fish pie tonight.'

And with that Eoin picked up his ball and shot out of the Gaelic grounds as fast as his legs could carry him.

CHAPTER 2

Later that evening, Dixie took down a bulky brown envelope from the bookcase and called Eoin over to the dining table.

'Andy posted these down to me last week, there's lots of you in action and a few of us old codgers up in the grandstand.' Andy Finn was an old friend and team-mate of Dixie's, who had helped him to get over his dislike of rugby and encouraged him to watch the game again.

'Look, there's one of me with Andy and my new photo album he gave me that day,' said Dixie. 'And here's one of us all with the trophy.'

Eoin picked up the group photograph and smiled – his mum, dad, grandad were all there, proud as punch as Eoin hugged the shining silver cup that he had played a large part in ensuring was currently sitting in the trophy cabinet up in Castlerock College.

'And here's one of you just about to kick the winning conversion …'

Eoin took the picture from his grandfather.

'It's a nice action shot,' said Dixie, 'but there's something wrong with the way it's been printed. There's a strange blur just under the posts there.'

Eoin peered into the image and, sure enough, a section just under the crossbar looked as if it was shimmering. And only Eoin knew why – he stared at the blurred patch, remembering that it was the very spot where his ghostly friend Brian had stood, encouraging him as he took the vital last minute kick.

Eoin had met Brian on a school tour to the Aviva Stadium and hadn't realised he was a ghost. They got chatting; Brian helped Eoin to learn the new sport and gave him great tips. It was only weeks later that he explained how he had been fatally injured during a match at the old stadium – and had continued to haunt it for almost a century. It took a bit of getting used to, but Eoin became very fond of his ghostly big brother.

'I don't know, Grandad, it's probably some flaw in the printing,' Eoin suggested, 'and the sun was doing funny things through the roof of the stadium that day – maybe it was that.'

Dixie shrugged, and passed on to the next photo.

'We'll have to have a couple of these framed, and put the rest in the album. I'd like that group shot for my wall; it brings back one of the best days I've had in forty years,' he smiled.

'And can I take that blurry one, please?' Eoin asked. 'It's a moment I'll never forget, but I still want to be reminded of it as often as possible.'

'OK, leave it there and I'll get a copy for you,' said Dixie. 'Now, tell me, when are you heading up to Dublin?'

'Sunday, Grandad, I think Dad's going to drive me up after lunch. Want to come for the ride?'

'That would be lovely. I'll see what your dad thinks, though. He's always fretting about me since my heart attack last year, and me in the peak of health and fitter than I've been for years.'

The night before Eoin was due to go back to school, Dylan knocked on his door.

'Howya, Eoin,' he mumbled, 'wanna go for a bit of walk?'

Eoin grabbed his hoodie and followed Dylan out the gate, catching up with him as they rounded the corner into the main street of Ormondstown.

'When you going up?' Dylan asked.

'Tomorrow afternoon. You OK for a lift? I'm not sure we'd have room.'

'Yeah, I'll be OK, I think. What's this school all about then?'

Eoin filled Dylan in on the way the school was structured, and how the school day and week worked for first years, especially for those who were new to the school. He explained the rugby set up, and told Dylan that he'd probably have to start on the third team, but he could work his way up quickly if he was any good. He explained his own experience of working his way up the teams and finishing the season by kicking the winning goal at Lansdowne Road.

'Are you a bit nervous?' asked Eoin.

'Not really,' said Dylan, 'We've always moved around a lot so I'm used to walking into brand new classrooms full of strangers. But there's a few things going on at home ....'

'Are you OK?'

'Yeah, I'll be fine. Just needed to get a bit of air. Fancy a bag of chips? It'll probably be boarding-school mushy peas from now on.'

Eoin joined Dylan in their last supper in Ormondstown before their migration next day.

As they walked back to Eoin's house a Garda car

cruised slowly up behind them.

'Take the hoodies off, lads,' came the call from the Garda.

The boys stopped and lowered their hoods. Eoin stood, shocked at being addressed in such a way for merely walking along the footpath. 'Is there something wrong?' he asked.

'No, nothing at all. Move along now,' came the reply.

The pair quickly turned the corner and stopped at the Madden family gate.

'That was a bit weird, wasn't it?' said Eoin.

'You get used to it,' said Dylan.

'Anyway, see you this time tomorrow up in Castlerock, have a good trip,' said Eoin, turning to go up the pathway.

'Yeah, I can't wait,' said Dylan, although from the look on his face he certainly didn't appear quite as enthusiastic as Eoin.

CHAPTER 3

Three generations of Maddens piled into the car next day, with a suitcase, rucksack and kitbag – all tightly-packed – filling up the boot. The drive from Ormondstown to Dublin usually took less than two hours, but Eoin's dad was the slowest driver in the country at the best of times. With a full load and Dixie's first long excursion for six months he was in danger of being overtaken by any moderately energetic tortoise. So the trip took far longer than it ought because his dad decided to stop every thirty miles for a bottle of water, or to get rid of a bottle of water, or to look at the view. Twilight was getting ready to make an appearance when they pulled into the grounds of Castlerock College.

'Not a lot has changed, has it?' said Dixie, looking up at the grey stone walls and the school motto carved over the doorway – "*Victoria Concordia Crescit*",' he read, '"Victory come through harmony". But it's been such a long time since I turned up here for the first day of term ...'

He stared all around as Dad pulled the car into the parking area, taking in the new buildings that lined the rear of the school. He tapped Eoin on the shoulder and pointed away to his right where the playing fields lay.

'See that, Eoin, that's where I used to practise my goal-kicking too. I never did more than fifty at one session though – no wonder you're twice as good as me!'

They got out of the car, and started to lift Eoin's luggage from the boot. With almost four months until the Christmas break, he needed an awful lot of supplies to get him through the term.

'Welcome back, Master Madden,' boomed out the voice of Mr McCaffrey, the genial headmaster of Castlerock. 'And a great welcome to our two former pupils as well!'

Mr McCaffrey strode down the steps and thrust his hand towards Eoin's grandad. 'Dixie Madden, welcome back to the Castlerock. Is it really six months since you last visited us? That was a truly memorable day, thanks mainly to young Madden Minor here, of course,' he said, clapping Eoin across the shoulders.

'You'll come in for a cup of tea and some sandwiches before the journey home, won't you?' he pressed.

The two senior Maddens agreed, and headed off to the headmaster's study.

'I'll be fine, it's no bother to lift three heavy bags up to the top floor on my own,' called out Eoin. 'I'll come down to say goodbye.'

'Ah, don't be such a moan, Eoin,' said Mr McCaffrey, 'and anyway, you're on the first floor this year, the rare privilege reserved for first-year students. There's a list of names on the wall there, you're in room ... seven.'

'Great,' harrumphed Eoin, only marginally happier. He carried the suitcase up to the first-floor landing.

As he returned for the rest of his luggage, he looked out the big open doorway and saw a small figure staggering up the long driveway. As the figure came closer, Eoin noticed that he was carrying a huge suitcase and a rucksack hung from his sagging shoulders. And as he reached the forecourt of the school Eoin recognised who it was.

'Dylan! Do you want a hand with that?' he asked.

'Eoin, great to see you. Yeah, could you take the suit-case?' Dylan replied.

The boys lugged the bags into the hallway where Eoin looked at his tiny Ormondstown Gaels team-mate.

Dylan looked like he was about to collapse.

'Are you all right, Dylan? How did you get here? Did you *walk* up the drive?'

Dylan looked at his feet.

'I did. I got the bus out from the city. It left me a couple of hundred metres from the gate.'

'And how did you get to Dublin?'

'Another bus. It was grand, plenty of room and I was able to have a snooze.'

'And you had to haul all that with you? Ah, Dylan, you should have said last night that you didn't have a lift, we would have worked something out.'

'Sure I was fine. Now, any idea where I'm supposed to be staying?' asked Dylan.

Eoin walked over to the list, and to their delight they found they had been billeted in the same dormitory. They struggled once again up the stairs under each of their burdens until they finally found room seven and pushed open the door.

'EOIN!' came a roar as a head popped up between two of the beds.

'Alan,' Eoin replied, 'You're not looking for your mouse down there again, are you?'

'No, I was just checking the beds – I'm first in so I get first choice. And a Father Geoghegan Cup medal gives you no extra privileges either,' Alan chuckled.

Eoin introduced his two pals to each other and they each picked out the bed that would be their resting place for the next nine months.

CHAPTER 4

'This is fierce lumpy,' complained Dylan as he gave his bed a quick test.

'They all are,' grumbled Alan. 'The mattresses are here since the days of Dixie Madden, I reckon.'

'Who's Dixie Madden?' asked Dylan.

'Ah, Dixie is the school's greatest legend,' answered Alan, 'grandfather of the school's latest legend ...' as he opened his arms and pointed at Eoin as if he was introducing a Hollywood star on a TV chat show.

'YOUR grandfather?' said Dylan, puzzled. 'What did he do?'

'Well,' muttered Eoin, 'he was a bit of a rugby star way back. Won the Senior Cup for Castlerock and could have played for Ireland, they say.'

'There's even a dormitory named after him upstairs,'

said Alan.

'And maybe they'll call this one after you, Eoin?' came the question from an elderly man who had just arrived in the doorway. 'Good evening all, and a special welcome to this young man – Mr Coonan, isn't it?'

'Yes, sir,' replied Dylan.

'I'm Andrew Finn, and I've been teaching here almost all my life, or so it feels like. But, sadly, I won't be getting the opportunity to teach you.'

'Why is that, sir?' asked Eoin.

'I've retired, Eoin,' said Mr Finn. 'That's what they call it when you stop working because the calendar says so. It's a bit of a shame, as I feel like I could go on for years yet.'

'That's terrible, sir. Is there no way they'll let you stay on?'

'Well, yes, I suppose there is, but I don't want to block a job for a new teacher coming into the profession. Mr McCaffrey has been very good about it, however, and has asked me to stay on as a sort of consultant to the History Department. He has quite a few plans for developing that area, and with the school's centenary coming up there'll be a book to write and archives to research. I certainly won't be idle!'

'And talking of Mr McCaffrey, it was he who told me

you were here, and to tell you that Dixie and your father are about to leave for Ormondstown. Do you want to come down and say goodbye?'

Eoin took the stairs two at a time and met the departing group as they were at the doorway to the school.

'Ah, Eoin, I'm glad we got a chance to say goodbye. Have a fantastic year here this year, and we'll catch up at Christmas. Actually, maybe you could let me know the results of your games. Could you text them to me?' asked Dixie.

'I can't, Grandad.' replied Eoin, 'I don't have a mobile phone.'

'Oh, well then, it's lucky I brought one along for you, isn't it?' Dixie said as he produced a shiny black phone from his pocket. 'It's full of "credits", I think they call them, and I even got your mum to put my number in it for you. So you've no excuse.'

'Oh Grandad, that's brilliant, of course I'll keep in touch …'

'Within the school rules, of course,' said Mr McCaffrey, 'I'll be explaining our guidelines on the use of mobiles at assembly tomorrow …'

'Of course,' said Eoin's dad. 'And now, we'd better be hitting the road. Have a good term, son, and it's good to know we can keep in touch a bit more. And remember

– rugby's all very well, but your books come first!'

'OK, Dad,' grinned Eoin. 'I'll go straight back to that Maths book I was reading upstairs. Safe home.'

'Oh, and I've something else, too,' said Dixie, handing Eoin a framed copy of the photograph he had wanted, the one of him about to kick the cup winning conversion.

'Thanks, Grandad, that's going on my locker,' he said.

As the car pulled away, Mr McCaffrey turned to Eoin.

'It's great to see Dixie looking so well. He was telling me you have been practising rugby over the summer too? You'll be glad to know we have a new rugby coach looking after the first years. He's actually from New Zealand, and played for the junior All Blacks. I think you'll like him.'

CHAPTER 5

The first day of term dawned with a loud hammering on the dormitory door. Eoin opened his eyes and lifted himself up on to his elbow to see what the ruckus was about.

'Half past seven, boys. Breakfast is in fifteen minutes and you need to be fully dressed and washed,' announced the human cockerel, the housemaster Mr Dwyer.

The occupants of room seven – who now numbered six after Rory, Kevin and Fiachra had arrived in dribs and drabs over the previous evening – rose as one, yawned and started digging their uniforms from their suitcases. Alan, who knew where the bottlenecks would build up in their morning routine, scarpered first to the washroom.

'Do you get a choice of breakfasts here?' Dylan asked

Eoin as they made their way downstairs.

'Yeah,' Eoin chuckled. 'You can eat, or you can starve.'

Sure enough, the breakfast menu pinned to the door consisted of just one line of text. 'Sausages (x2)' it read.

Alan, who liked his food, grumbled 'How do they expect us to grow when this is all we get?'

'It's two sausages more than I got in my old school, in fairness,' grinned Dylan, 'but I'll get you another one, watch this.'

When he got to the top of the queue he smiled at the canteen worker who was doling out breakfast.

'Is your name Coonan, by any chance?' he asked. 'It's just that you remind me very much of my mother, only you're much younger looking of course.'

'Ah no, pet, my name is Miss Collins, and I'm from just down the road, all my life. You're new, aren't you?'

'Yes, I'm up from Tipperary,' sighed Dylan, 'I miss home and my mum and sister.'

'Ah, we'll look after you, pet,' said Miss Collins, slipping an extra sausage and slice of toast onto his plate.

'Thanks a lot,' grinned Dylan, returning her wink.

At the long table Dylan transferred the surplus goodies to a grateful Alan's plate. The boys munched their breakfast and cast their eyes around the room to see who else had returned to school.

Anton came over to say hello and tell them he had stayed back a year in Sixth Class as they had realised he was too young – and that he was back in the Dixie Madden Dormitory.

'It's not so bad,' he said, 'I'm the oldest in the year now, instead of the youngest, so I get a bit more respect!'

The boys laughed at Anton and promised to keep in touch.

'Did I take his place?' asked Dylan.

'Yeah, I suppose you did,' said Eoin, 'But don't worry, your feet aren't half as smelly as his and your sausage-scamming skills are impressive, so you're already a popular arrival.'

'Uh-oh,' said Alan, 'here comes trouble.'

Eoin gave Dylan a dig in the ribs as two boys strode up the middle of the hall, pausing only to steal a sausage from one of the younger boys' plates.

'That's Richie Duffy,' he hissed. 'Nasty piece of work, well worth steering clear of.'

Duffy stopped at the table Eoin and Dylan were seated at.

'Hi, Eoin,' he smiled. 'And who's this new recruit?'

'Hi, Richie,' said Eoin, suspiciously,. 'This is Dylan, he's in our dorm.'

'Hi, Dylan, are you any good at rugby?'

'Not too bad,' said Dylan. 'I didn't play last year, but I played a bit down in Limerick before that.'

'Great, I look forward to seeing you out at training tomorrow. We're having a run out and then the First Year trials are on next week. You be there too, Eoin? Talk to you then.'

And with that, Duffy walked to the back of the room, pausing to grab another sausage from a fifth-class boy's plate before he sat down with this sidekick Ollie Flanagan.

'He seems OK,' said Dylan. 'But what's wrong Eoin, you look shocked? he asked.

'I don't believe it, that's the first time he's ever spoken a civil word to me. He tried to make my life miserable all last year – and he succeeded in doing so for loads of other lads. He's the biggest bully in the year, but now he's suddenly come over all friendly. That's why I'm shocked.'

'Yeah!' said Alan. 'He picked on you more than anyone but you stood up to him and he laid off. I suppose winning the cup single-handed means he can't really take you on again – you're Mr Popular this year. Didn't you see how all the younger kids look at you like you're Jonny Sexton?'

'I don't know, I'm suspicious though,' said Eoin.

'And why is he going around inviting people to rugby training? They haven't named him captain again *yet*,' said Rory.

'Maybe he's just trying to look like he's captain so he gets the job?' said Fiachra.

'Yeah, that could be it,' said Eoin.

'And why was he so keen about whether you play rugby, Dylan?' Rory asked.

'I don't know, maybe they're stuck for a classy scrum-half?' replied the new boy.

The table went quiet, and Rory frowned.

'I'm not sure about that.' Rory said, '*I'm* the scrum-half.'

CHAPTER 6

After breakfast the entire school assembled in the great hall to hear Mr McCaffrey's annual welcome speech. Eoin shuffled awkwardly from foot to foot, trying to avoid Alan who was making faces at him as the headmaster droned on.

'… and, as I said to Master Madden last night …'

Eoin jumped at the mention of his name, and went pink as he realised half the school was now staring at him.

'… we have a new school policy on mobile phone use, of which you must take great heed. Day boys may carry a phone into school, but it must be switched to silent at all times, and must not be answered under any circumstances. Our policy can be summed up as "We don't want to see them, and we don't want to hear them." If we do see or hear a boy with a phone out, it will be confiscated for one week and stored in my safe.

'Boarding pupils may not carry the phone out of their house, and to do so will also result in confiscation. They may use them at specified times, which vary from year to year, which you will be told by your housemaster. When you are out of the house you must leave them in your locker, switched off.

'We have provided free wi-fi this year, and will be monitoring your internet activity. Mobile phones are a great boon, but can be an awful nuisance too, so obey our rules.'

Mr McCaffrey finished up by welcoming all the new boys, and gave the usual message about how rugby was the great unifying agent for Castlerock boys, past and present, and how he expected this year to be even more glorious than the last.

'Yawn, yawn, yawn,' said Alan as they wandered off to their classrooms. 'Everyone knows we won't win the Junior Cup until the great Eoin Madden gets to be old enough to play. I bet they'll try to forge your birth cert.'

'Are you really any good?' Dylan asked, but Eoin just shrugged his shoulders and said 'Well, I had a bit of a good run last year and I enjoyed the place-kicking, but don't mind that eejit.'

When they walked into their classroom, they were surprised to see Mr Finn standing at the head of the class with a much younger man.

'Good morning, boys, hurry on there and get to your seats,' he said.

When the boys had settled, Mr Finn began to speak.

'Well, it is good to have you all back at Castlerock, and a few bright new faces too, I see. I'm afraid I won't have the honour of teaching you this year, but I will still be around and will take you occasionally I'm sure. Your new teacher is this gentleman, Mr Lawson, who comes from the far side of the world. If I say the phrase "All Black" you may have a clue to his origins!'

'Is he from Africa, sir?' answered Fiachra.

'No, not at all. He's from New Zealand, or the "Land of the Long White Cloud" as the Maori call it,' said Mr Finn. 'By a coincidence it's also the place where your new rugby coach Mr McRae is from too. Mr Lawson will be teaching you history this year, and I know he is keen to commence his first job in Ireland, so I'll hand you over now with a request to be on your best behaviour and most attentive for him.'

The new teacher looked around the room, taking in the faces of the boys.

'Thank you, Mr Finn, and good morning, guys. I'm

Greg Lawson, and I'm from a place called Wellington, which is the capital of New Zealand. I've come to Dublin through an exchange programme between my school and Castlerock, and I really look forward to teaching you this year.

'Let me assure you I have long been a student of Irish history, so you won't be missing out there. I also hear you're all really keen on the subject, which doesn't surprise me when I hear that you have been taught by Mr Finn last year.

'You have three main periods to study this year, and we'll be doing some projects on them all, so I hope you're all keen for some extra work too. Any questions?'

'Sir, did you ever see the All Blacks play?' asked Charlie Johnston, one of Eoin's team-mates on the victorious Under-13 team the year before.

'We-e-e-ll,' Mr Lawson began, 'it might surprise you to hear that not everybody in New Zealand is a rugby nut. Yeah, of course I've seen the All Blacks – we did win the last World Cup, didn't we? – but I'm more of a soccer and cricket man myself. Do they play that here?'

'Not in Castlerock,' said Charlie.

'That's a shame, maybe we'll get something together,' said Mr Lawson. 'Anyway, nice try Master Johnston, but we're not here to talk sport – let's open the books on page one ...'

CHAPTER 7

After lessons Eoin and Dylan went back to the dormitory to collect their rugby gear.

'What did you think of that?' asked Eoin.

'Not too bad at all,' replied Dylan. 'The teachers seem really nice and a few of the lads were friendly enough. They all speak with a funny accent though.'

'Yeah, and they say we culchies have a weird accent too!' said Eoin. 'I couldn't work that out last year. But sure you get used to it.'

When they reached the pitch they tied up their boots and jogged over to the rest of the boys who were doing stretches with Mr Carey.

'Good afternoon, Mr Madden,' he said, checking his watch, 'And with forty-five seconds to spare – that's your closest yet. Keep an eye on that – hero of the

Geoghegan Cup or not ...'

'Sorry, sir, my locker was stuck,' Eoin replied.

'And who is this new guy?' asked the coach.

'Dylan Coonan,' replied the boy.

Mr Carey asked him about his rugby experience, and raised his eyebrows when Dylan mentioned the well-known Limerick club he had played with as an Under-12.

The group – all three Under-14 teams – had a very light run-out, shaking the cobwebs out of their legs after a mostly lazy summer.

'You're looking fit, Madden,' Mr Carey said, as the session wound down.

'Yes, sir, I'm fairly sharp after a summer playing Gaelic. That's where I met Dylan,' he explained.

'Careful you don't burn yourself out with round-the-year sport, though. The Leinster branch has new rules about that this year.'

He addressed the whole group: 'Listen guys, the old boys' club were delighted that you won the Father Geoghegan Cup last term. There were a lot of them there that day to see Leinster and they were really proud that their old school did so well. A couple of them organised a collection and they've raised some money to make a presentation to you all. They've invited you into the Aviva Stadium next week for a reception, with a bite to eat and some refreshments.

'It's a very nice thing for them to do and I want you all on your best behaviour and properly turned-out on Monday after school. We'll bring you there and back on the minibus. The invite is for the whole year, although there'll only be presentations to the squad who were picked for the final. Is everyone OK to go? Great, I'll see you Wednesday for a more serious run-out, when your new coach will be here ...

'Oh yeah, don't look so surprised, didn't I mention that I'm moving up to the Junior Cup Team? Well, your new coach is a Kiwi, and a serious rugby player in his day too. He played for the Junior All Blacks, but he's come over on a coach-exchange programme and will be looking after the Seniors and the Under-14s all year. He missed his flight from London this morning so you won't get to see him till Wednesday.'

'Will you be going to New Zealand, sir?' asked Rory.

'Eh, sadly no,' said Mr Carey. '"New-Bridge" is as far as I'll be going this year!'

CHAPTER 8

By Wednesday the new coach had landed, and had already caused a bit of a stir around Castlerock. He wasn't very tall, but had long blond hair and a scruffy beard, giving him the appearance more of a Viking than a man from the Southern Pacific. He wore jeans and a day-glo t-shirt, even with the Irish weather starting to turn a little chilly.

But when the Under-14s arrived for training after school that day, he was dressed in a sharp black tracksuit with a tiny silver fern on the chest.

'G'day boys, my name is Nathan McRae, and I'm here to coach you rugby this year. I hear you're pretty good already – judging by that beaut trophy sitting in the cabinet in Mr McCaffrey's office. We'll have a bit of a run on the paddock today, and get down to some hard graft soon, but with a bit of luck she'll be right real soon. I'm totally stoked to be here.'

The boys stared at Mr McRae.

'You OK?' he asked. 'Was it something I said? Did you understand any of it?'

'Eh, it certainly sounded like English, sir,' said Rory, 'but it didn't make much sense to me ...' as the rest of the group nodded.

'Fair enough,' said the coach. 'I'll try to keep it simple then. Jog up and down the field there to get loose. Oh yes, and can Duffy and Madden stand over there please.'

Everyone stared as Richie and Eoin were directed to the corner of the field, but the group started their warm-up jog as the new coach wandered over to the duo.

'OK, guys,' he started, 'I'm keen to appoint a captain for this team from the get-go. And I believe in leading a team from the front and by example. I've talked to Mr Carey and he tells me you two are the best players we've got. Is that true?'

'Yes,' said Duffy, without hesitation.

'Well ...' said Eoin.

'OK. I'm glad to hear you are so confident in your own ability, Duffy. I like that in a player – and a skipper. But why are you being so modest, Madden?' the coach asked. 'Is it not true that you won the cup for us virtually single-handed this year?'

'I'm not arguing that I'm *not* one of the best players, sir.' Eoin retorted, 'It's just I don't think Richie is one too.'

Richie Duffy looked stunned.

'I see what you did there, Madden,' said Mr McRae. 'Now, look, are you quite sure of what you say?'

'Yes, sir,' said Eoin. 'Richie's a good player, but he's not in the top two in the team. I think if you're looking for a captain, you should look at Charlie Johnston, who plays lock.'

'OK,' said Mr McRae, 'I'll have to think about this and watch the DVD of the final again. I was impressed with you when you moved up to first five-eighth after Duffy got injured …'

Eoin looked puzzled.

'Oh sorry, I forgot you guys have different names for positions – "first five-eighth" is what we call your out-half.

'Anyway, I also believe that the crucial spine of the team is where the best leaders are – hooker, number eight, out-half, full-back – so I'll be looking closely at all those positions from the get-go. Go and join your squad and we'll talk about this later.'

Eoin and Richie jogged towards the far end of the pitch where the Under-14As and 14Bs were still doing their warm-up.

'You're a rat, Madden,' spat Duffy. 'Who do you think you are dissing *me*. I've been the best player on that team since we started playing five years ago.'

'Sorry, Richie, nothing personal, I just don't see it that way,' replied Eoin.

'I was even getting to like you a bit,' Duffy hissed, 'but if the gloves are off, then I'm up for a scrap too.'

'Like I said, it was nothing personal,' said Eoin.

CHAPTER 9

The first week at school flew past, and Eoin and Dylan settled quickly into life in Castlerock. At the weekend Eoin took Dylan on a tour of the grounds, showing him the best hiding places and the best windows in which to sit to catch the last of the sun's rays. Dylan even started going about on his own, which was a relief to Eoin who didn't really want to spend the whole school year with a Siamese twin.

After lessons on Monday the whole year trooped onto two mini buses parked just outside the headmaster's office. Mr Carey climbed on board and stood at the top of the bus in which Eoin was sitting with his friends.

'Right boys, a bit of quiet please. This is a rare treat for Castlerock rugby, and I hope you enjoy the day and appreciate it. I know you understand how you need to behave so I won't go on about it.

'When we get to the Aviva we will go straight to the committee room where we will watch a DVD of last year's final and have some snacks and drinks. Then the old boys want to present you with a memento of the occasion. Enjoy the day and – like I said the last time we went there – make me proud.'

Dylan was clearly excited as the bus made its way through the traffic towards Lansdowne Road. 'I've never been here before,' he admitted. 'I'd love to see a big match in the Aviva, I can't imagine what it was like to actually *play* there.'

'It was a bit special,' agreed Eoin, 'but it's funny how easy it is to shut off everything when the match is going on. I only really panicked towards the end, just in time for the last kick of the game!'

'But they all lived happily after, so you got over it quickly then,' quipped Dylan.

The bus pulled into the tunnel that ran all the way around the inside of the stadium, and parked in an area where the passageway widened.

The boys were greeted by a woman in a stadium jacket and escorted to a lift which took them to the fourth level. The room was lined with tables crammed with goodies, but the Castlerock boys remembered their teacher's warning so they waited for the order to eat.

A recording of the final was playing on a big screen, and Dylan was among the boys keenly watching the action.

'That's really cool, Eoin,' he told him. 'You're a pretty good player. But I'd say I'd have a good chance of getting on as scrum-half. He's not up to much, is he?'

'Careful now, Dylan. Rory's one of our room-mates and he's a good pal. See how it goes – but you might have to take your time,' Eoin replied.

'Why?' asked Dylan. 'There's a new coach. He'll pick the best man for the job, surely?'

'Maybe …' said Eoin, who couldn't fault Dylan's argument, but he could also see it would mean trouble ahead in room seven.

'Attention, everybody,' called out a man in a grey suit. 'My name is Paddy Murray, and it is an awful long time since I played Under-13 for Castlerock College. I'm chairman this year of the old boys' club, and we decided to honour your remarkable victory in this very stadium last season. It was a stunning performance and we were very proud of you that day, especially with so many people here to watch it.

'We would like to make a presentation to each member of that marvellous side, and I would like to invite the the inspirational captain, Richard Duffy, to come up and call out their names.'

Richie joined Mr Murray at the top of the room, and began to read out the names of the team.

'Hugh Bowers, Glen Fox, Harry Young ...' and on he went, working his way through the squad. Each player was presented with a team photo and a classy dark green tracksuit with his name embroidered on the back and the legend 'Fr Geoghegan Cup winners' on the chest.

Duffy went through the team in order of shirt number, but missed out the Number 15. When he had finished with the replacements, he called out his own name, collected his prize, and walked back to his friends at the back of the hall.

There was a round of applause before Mr Murray put his hand up. 'Hang on a second,' he said. 'There's one tracksuit left over ... Let me check ... yes, the name on the back is "Madden". Is he not here? Has he left the school?'

'No, sir.' said Eoin, 'I'm right here. Maybe Richie forgot I was playing that day.'

Duffy glared at Eoin, but if his omission was a deliberate snub, it certainly didn't work. As Eoin walked up to receive his memento, the applause and cheering was louder than for all the other boys put together.

CHAPTER 10

After a couple more speeches the boys settled back to watch the dramatic second half of the game, or to wander around the trophy-filled room and stare at the photographs of the sport's greatest warriors from years gone by.

'Congratulations, Eoin, that was a lovely prize to get, wasn't it?' asked Mr Finn.

'Yes, sir, thank you,' he replied.

Mr Finn pointed at one of the photographs on the wall. 'That's the first team to visit here from New Zealand, in 1905 I think,' he said. 'The captain of that time was a very special player, although I don't see him in the photo. Ah, here's Mr McRae, he may be able to tell you about him …'

'Hello, Mr Finn,' the new coach replied. 'And well

done, Eoin, I'm impressed watching the game there.'

'Tell me,' asked the older teacher, 'do you know much about this All Black team?'

'I do indeed,' said Mr McRae, his eyes lighting up as he looked at the picture, which had become yellowed with time.

'They were the first team to be called the All Blacks – the Originals we call them back home. They were a phenomenal unit, led by an amazing man called Dave Gallaher, who believe it or not was born in Ireland …'

'Really?' said Eoin. 'Why was he playing for New Zealand then?'

'Well, I'm not sure of the details, but I think his family immigrated to New Zealand when he was a baby. That was an amazing journey to take at the time, sailing in a steam ship which took months. He grew up to be one of our greatest players, and wrote the best book about playing the game that I've ever read. My first coach told me he thought it was the start of modern rugby coaching and I can't argue with that.

'His story is still remembered in New Zealand though because he lost his life in the First World War. When I was still playing I had a season in Auckland and we got to the final of the Dave Gallaher Shield. I'm glad to see he's not forgotten in his native land too.'

'Well that's an amazing story,' said Mr Finn. 'I must look him up on the Google-machine in the staff room. And he was from Ireland, you say?'

'Yeah, a place called Donny-gal, is it?'

'Ah yes, Donegal. We pronounce it "Dunny-gawl" here.'

'It's funny that he's not in this picture.' said Mr McRae, 'Maybe you could find out why on the Google-thing too, Mr Finn?'

Eoin laughed and excused himself before he wandered over to where his friends were tucking into the last of the chicken goujons and cocktail sausages.

'That was a great dig at Duffy,' said Alan, 'He totally tried to blank you but you ended up an even bigger legend.'

'Yeah, well I decided this summer I'm not going to stand for any rubbish from Duffy any more. Bullies like him just need to be taken on. He's a coward really, and I think if we all stand together and stand up to him he won't be able to bully us all.

'I even told Mr McRae that he wouldn't make a good captain this year. I told him in front of Duffy too. I think that shocked him a bit – that's why he was trying to get back at me today.'

'Wow, Eoin, that was brave,' said Rory, who like most

of the boys had been one of Duffy's victims. 'You'll want to watch your back, though. He'll try to get at you in other ways.'

'Whatever,' said Eoin, with a grin. 'You heard the cheer – I've got the guys behind me. I'll be all right.'

CHAPTER 11

As the boys marched back to their bus, Eoin tapped Alan on the shoulder.

'That's where it all started, that's where I first met Brian,' he said, pointing to the corridor that led to the treatment room.

'Who's Brian?' asked Alan.

Eoin reddened as he realised he had blurted out his secret, distracted by the excitement of the evening and the return to the scene of the most amazing days of his life.

'Eh … eh … I mean … where we went on the stadium tour …' Eoin stammered, unconvincingly.

'You mentioned some guy called Brian before. What's that all about?' asked Alan.

Eoin stopped and looked at his feet.

'OK, but it's a long story, and a bit unbelievable, really,' he said, 'but I'll tell you all about it later.'

'Hmmm,' said Alan, looking quizzically at his friend. OK, how about a stroll around the grounds when we get back. I need to work all that pizza off,' he said, slapping his belly.

The rugby players climbed back onto the bus for the journey back to Castlerock. Eoin sat quietly at the back with Alan, and the pair were a bit surprised to see Richie Duffy and Dylan get on the bus together, laughing and joking.

'What's Duffy up to, I wonder?' mused Alan. 'He'd usually have the new boy crying in the corner by now.'

'Dylan wants Rory's place on the team,' replied Eoin. 'It looks like he thinks sucking up to the captain is the best way to do it.'

'Oooh, that could get very messy!' said Alan. 'Being on the first-fifteen means everything to Rory. Our little dorm mightn't be so happy if Dylan takes his place.'

'I know, but Dylan is tough. I'm afraid his ambition could be a problem for us all.'

The return bus journey passed peacefully, interspersed with guffaws from Duffy and Dylan who seemed to be getting on like a house on fire.

Eoin gave Fiachra his tracksuit and asked him to leave

it in the dorm, before he and Alan set off at a jog for the playing fields. Once they got there Eoin sprinted the length of the field with Alan puffing along far behind. The friends lay on the ground till their breath returned to a steady pace.

'So what's all this mystery?' Alan gasped.

'Seriously, you have to promise not to tell *anyone*, or tell me I'm an idiot,' Eoin pleaded. 'But I can't explain it, just that what I'm telling you is completely true.'

'OK, I promise, go on,' said Alan, now completely mystified.

'Brian is a ghost—' Eoin started.

Alan laughed. 'A ghost? Ah, come *on*, Eoin, you must think *I'm* an idiot.'

'No, I'm deadly serious,' he replied. 'I met him in the Aviva last year, and we became friends. He gave me some really good tips about rugby, even during the final.

'He was an old player who was killed playing rugby in the ground years ago, and came back to, sort of, haunt the place ever since. He's gone now though, the last time I saw him was just after we won the final.'

Alan just stared at his best friend. His mouth opened and closed a couple of times as he tried to ask one of the many questions he wanted to ask. They all came at a rush.

'Was he, like, white like a sheet, or all gory like a zombie?'

'How was he killed?'

'And how did you see him?'

'Hang on, hang on,' said Eoin. 'He looked like any rugby player in his kit, but the jersey and boots looked very old-fashioned. He looked a bit pale, I suppose, but there was no blood. He was a prop and got injured when a scrum collapsed. I still don't know why I was able to see and hear him – he told me that he'd been around for more than eighty years and I was the first person able to see him and that he was able to talk to.

'He was a really nice lad, very friendly but a bit lonely I suppose. I sneaked in here a few times to talk to him. He was a great help. I hope I'll be OK this year without his advice.'

'Ah, don't say that, Eoin,' Alan chipped in. 'You were epic last year, ghost advice or not.'

Alan tapped his toe against the goalpost. 'I'll tell you Eoin, that story is a bit hard to take in to be honest … But I *do* believe you, even if no one else would. I'd love to see a ghost,' he went on. 'Is there any chance he might reappear if we went back to the Aviva?'

'I don't think so,' replied Eoin. 'On the day of the final he said he was going to leave and there was no sign of him there today.'

'It's not fair,' grumbled Alan, 'Nothing interesting ever happens to me.'

'I don't know. One day you might beat me in the race back,' laughed Eoin, as he took off in the direction of the school.

CHAPTER 12

Next day the first years had Mr Lawson for history. At the end of the class he told them that, at Mr Finn's suggestion, they were going to enter the Young Historian of the Year competition for the first time. This was a very prestigious award scheme that included a generous prize for both the school and the winning pupil, including a trip for a class group to a historic site anywhere in Europe.

'Mr Finn tells me you have some excellent young historians among you,' said Mr Lawson, 'but I want everyone to have a go at this. Have a think about what you'd like to write about and we'll start tying ideas down at our next class.'

'Yawn,' said Alan as the boys wandered off to do their after-school work.

'I don't know,' said Eoin, 'I like history. It could be a bit of crack. It'll give us an excuse to get some extra time on the computer.'

After they finished their homework they kicked a ball back and forth a few dozen times before Eoin called a halt to the game.

'I'm going to go to the library. I want to check out if they have a book. Want to come?'

'No, I'm whacked,' said Alan. 'I'm going to crash out on my bed.'

Eoin jogged over to the main building, and slipped into the school library, which was on the ground floor beside Mr McCaffrey's office.

Besides the librarian, a retired English teacher called Mr McDonagh, he was alone.

'Can I help you?' the librarian asked.

'Yes, sir,' replied Eoin. 'I'm looking for a book called *The Complete Rugby Footballer*. It's by an old guy who played for New Zealand. I can't remember his name, sorry.'

'Hmmm, that's interesting. We have a lot of books about rugby, but I'm not sure I've heard of that one. Let me check the catalogue.'

The grey-haired man thumbed his way through a big box full of small white cards. After some minutes, he pulled one out.

'Yes, here it is. *The Complete Rugby Footballer* by D. Gallaher and W.J. Stead. Gosh, published in 1906! I hope it's not too fragile to read,' he murmured. 'Follow me ...'

The librarian took off towards the far corner of the library, where a dusty cabinet with a glass-panelled front stood. He selected a small key from an enormous bunch and opened the door with a creak. He reached inside and carefully lifted down a thick, brown book which he handed to Eoin.

'Take good care of that, young man, I doubt it has been looked at in a hundred years. It is not available to borrow, I'm afraid, so you will have to read it here. And as I'm closing up in ten minutes you had better be quick.'

Eoin sat down at a desk and examined the cover of the book. The title and names of the authors were picked out in gold and Eoin had to wipe a layer of dust off the spine before he opened it.

He examined a photograph on the first page, a side shot of a grinning rugby player holding a ball. Opposite was the title again, and above it a message written neatly in ink. Eoin read it, and suddenly shivered as if some-one had opened a window and an icy blast of wind had blown through the old room.

There, in the top corner, were written the words 'B.F. Hanrahan, from Charlie, Christmas 1927'.

Eoin stared wide-eyed at the page, and looked up to where the librarian was busy tidying away some volumes.

'Brian …' he started, 'But how …'

'I was wondering that myself,' came a whisper behind him.

Eoin turned quickly, and there leaning against a bookcase was a pale young man dressed in black, red and yellow hooped rugby kit.

'Brian!' he gasped, at which the librarian looked up.

'Are you all right, young man?' he asked. 'You must keep quiet, even if there are no other readers about.'

'I'm sorry,' said Eoin. 'I just got a bit of a surprise.'

'*Surprise*? Huh, it didn't seem like that sort of book,' grumped the librarian.

Eoin put his head down, and whispered out of the side of his mouth, 'How did you get here? Where have you been?'

'I'm not sure how I got here,' said Brian. 'It must have been that book. Maybe it works like Aladdin's lamp? I got that book from my brother on the last Christmas Day I was alive.

'I was really interested in the All Blacks and the way they changed the game. I had seen them play Ireland in

Lansdowne Road a year or two before and they were very impressive.

'I remember after I died that my brothers packed up all my belongings and sold off what they didn't want as keepsakes. They raised enough to buy a trophy which they donated to the club for best young player, or something of that order. Someone in the school must have bought that book and it ended up here after that ...'

'Time's up!' came the call from the librarian. 'I'm open again tomorrow after school if you need to consult the book again. I'll keep it here under the counter for you.'

Eoin stood and turned to say goodbye to Brian, but the ghost had already departed.

CHAPTER 13

The Under-14 trials were very well attended – even some of the boys who hadn't played rugby the year before turned out, eager to sample this sport that had so enthralled Castlerock at the Aviva Stadium the previous year.

Mr Carey was there too, and organised the dividing up of the players into four teams, but Mr McRae took the two best teams and led them up to the senior pitch to play a twenty-minute-a-side game. The A selection to play the Bs consisted of the starting fifteen from the Fr Geoghegan Cup final, so Eoin slotted in at inside centre, Richie Duffy at out-half and Rory was scrum-half.

As a new boy, Dylan couldn't have expected any better than to be put on the C team to take on the Ds, but even so he was a bit miffed.

Most of the players were a bit rusty, but Eoin's summer spent playing Gaelic stood to him and he made a couple of good breaks and one glorious sidestepping run that resulted in a try under the posts.

'Nice work, Madden,' called Mr McRae, 'take your kick over here by the touchline. It's too easy under the posts.'

Eoin was a bit irked that his good work to get under the post was being disregarded, but he didn't complain, and walked over to where Mr McRae was standing. He placed the ball carefully, and with a short run and effortless kick, hoisted the ball high over the bar, neatly bisecting the white timbers.

'Wow, I like your style,' said Mr McRae. 'You must practise that a lot.'

'Yes, sir,' Eoin replied. 'I kept it up over the summer down home.'

'Great, that's serious application. Now back to your position.'

Both games were being played simultaneously, so when half-time came, Mr Carey strolled over to talk to Mr McRae.

'That kid from Limerick is a pretty good scrum-half,' he said, quietly. 'It might be worth giving him a half on the Bs – David Vincent is no great shakes and Coonan could definitely challenge Rory Grehan for a place.'

'OK,' replied Mr McRae, 'I agree with you about Vincent, but I think Grehan shows a bit of guts.'

Mr Carey sent Dylan up to the senior pitch, and the new boy arrived with a grin as wide as the River Shannon.

'Howya, lads,' he said as he took his place. 'I'm Dylan and I'm pretty good at this. Just make sure I get lots of ball.'

The B team stared at this brash newcomer, whose cockiness seemed even more comical because he was barely up to shoulder height on any of them.

Rory looked across at Eoin as he prepared to restart the second half. He wasn't at all happy.

In the next break in play Eoin put his hand on Rory's shoulder. 'Relax, Rory, you're the man in possession. We all know what you can do and you have a Geoghegan Cup medal to prove it.'

'Thanks, Eoin, but that doesn't mean much when the coach was on the other side of the world when we won it,' he replied, glumly.

The A team found their form in the second half, and thanks to some quick passing by Rory to Richie Duffy, who made some good kicks into their opponents' corners, they recorded an easy win.

After the games were over, Mr McRae called the four teams around him.

'Right, gentlemen, that was a very impressive bit of rugby for so early in the new season. I'm seriously impressed with how well organised you guys are, and I'm very confident we can continue our winning ways over the winter. I've been concentrating on the top end of the talent pool, but I am going to take a keen and close interest in how all the teams get on.

'I put great store in having the right men in the right jobs on the team, so I will be talking to a few of you about maybe changing positions. But right now I just want to announce that I have selected a boy to be captain this year, and that I believe he has the ability and leadership qualities to be a great skipper. I want you all to row in behind him, and give him your support because it's never an easy job. I'd like him to come up here and say a few words about what sort of captain he wants to be. Come on up, Eoin Madden!'

Eoin stopped, and his mouth opened, soundlessly. He tried hard not to look across where Richie was standing, but he just couldn't resist it and was rewarded with a thunderous glare.

He stepped up beside Mr McRae, who shook his hand and pointed out at the seventy boys who were watching events closely.

'Tell them, Eoin. You're in charge,' he said.

'Em, em, well …' Eoin didn't know what to say. He looked down at Alan, Dylan and Rory, who had huge grins on their faces.

'Well, thank you, sir, for giving me this big job. I'm very honoured to get it, and well, I hope I can live up to what you want from us. I hope you all enjoy playing for the school this year and work really hard in training. We have some great players here and lots of competition so I hope the Bs and Cs work hard too. I started last year on the Cs so anyone can do it.'

He stopped speaking and walked back to where his friends stood.

'Thanks, Eoin,' said Mr McRae, 'And now we'll have each of the teams breaking up and working on fitness …'

CHAPTER 14

When training was over, Rory and Alan sought out Eoin and walked towards the changing rooms together.

'That's amazing, Eoin,' said Alan.

'Yeah,' said Rory, 'it's great news. I suppose my place will be safe on the first team now!'

Eoin stopped and looked at Rory. 'Sorry, Rory, you can't presume that. The coach will pick the team, but although I'll probably have a say, I just can't show you any favours. We have to pick the best team.'

Rory bit his lip and glowered, before jogging ahead of the other pair.

'I knew that was going to be trouble,' sighed Eoin. 'Dylan wasn't bad today, but I'd definitely stick with Rory for the moment. I hope Mr McRae agrees with me.'

At that moment, Dylan caught up with them. 'Well, skipper, what did you think? I'm pretty good, amn't I?' he asked, buzzing around the pair like an oversized wasp.

'Yeah, you're really good,' admitted Eoin, 'but like I told Rory, I won't be picking the teams. Everyone's just got to work hard in training and I'm sure Mr McRae will be fair.'

'OK, I can handle that,' said Dylan. 'Rory's a nice guy but I'm definitely better and I haven't played for more than a year. A bit more practice and I'll be ready to take him.'

'Well, if that's what you think,' muttered Eoin, 'but keep me out of it. I have to live with the two of you.'

Alan piped up, 'Don't worry, Eoin, I certainly won't be pressuring you for a place on the first-fifteen. I dropped the ball every time it came to me on the Ds. I'll be lucky if they ask me back to training ...'

'It takes all sorts, Alan, and the crack is good down on the Cs and Ds,' said Eoin, consoling his pal. 'You never know when a dose of the measles might break out and you'll find yourself on the Junior Cup team.'

Alan went white. 'Oh no, you don't think that's possible, do you?'

'It's possible,' said Eoin, 'but there's about a hundred and fifty lads who'd need to be sick before they'd have to call on you!'

Eoin ducked as Alan aimed a playful slap at his head, and dodged into the dressing room before the wounded winger could try again.

Later, after tea, Eoin and Alan wandered down to the common room to watch a soccer match on TV.

'Mr Lawson says he's more of a soccer man – do you think he was talking about starting a team?' asked Alan. 'I reckon I'd be a lot better at that than rugby.'

'Well, why don't you ask him?' said Eoin. 'But I'd say McCaffrey and the rest of them wouldn't be too keen on anything that might distract from rugby.'

'Still, there's a load of guys interested in football, and if they can't get on any of the three league and cup teams, it wouldn't cut across,' argued Alan. 'I'm going to ask Mr Lawson in the morning.'

'OK,' said Eoin, 'but I won't have time to play that AND rugby—'

'Who asked you to?' butted in Alan. 'We'd need to have a hundred and fifty guys down with the measles before you'd be selected for the Castlerock United FC first eleven!'

'Aha, you got me there,' laughed Eoin, 'got me good.'

CHAPTER 15

Next morning, Mr Lawson was in a very good mood when he walked into the First Year classroom.

'Right, boys,' he beamed, 'today is the day we decide on our projects for the Young Historian competition. I presume you have all decided what your subject is going to be?'

He was greeted by five rows of faces that each started blank, then turned pink, before ending with expressions which told of various degrees of panic.

'Ah, I understand. OK, well let's work out a few ideas and we'll have you all sorted before the class is over. Who prefers Irish history?'

A handful of hands went up, and after Mr Lawson made a few suggestions the boys agreed on the individual subjects for their projects.

He worked his way around the class, eventually ensuring all the boys had a topic to work on. The last name on the list was Eoin's and Mr Lawson stood by his desk.

'Right, Madden, what's it going to be? You haven't shown any interest in any of the characters or events we talked about up to this.'

Eoin stared back at the teacher. He had missed most of the class daydreaming – his new responsibility and the return of Brian had distracted him from the lesson.

'Well, is there anyone in history that you'd like to research?' asked Mr Lawson.

'Yes, sir,' said Eoin, thinking quickly. 'I was reading about this famous Irishman who was killed during the First World War and I thought he might be interesting.'

'Hmmm, that can be a very good period to research,' replied the teacher. 'What's your character's name?'

'Dave Gallaher,' said Eoin, 'He played rugby for New Zea—'

'I know exactly who he is,' interrupted Mr Lawson, 'And I agree he was a very interesting man. But whether he is a suitable case for study I'm not so sure. It's not a sports-essay competition.'

'I've already dug out his book in the library,' said Eoin, hoping his apparent enthusiasm might encourage the teacher.

'Really? All right, but keep the rugby part of this to

the minimum,' he said. 'It's not a sports-writing class we're doing. Stick to his life story and his time as a soldier.'

'I will, sir. When is the project due?'

Mr Lawson returned to the top of the class.

'Now, young men, your attention please. You have all agreed on the subjects you are going to research. You will have five weeks from today to compile your information, and then we will spend two weeks writing up your essays. The closing date for the competition is just after the Halloween break, so I want you to kick into this as soon as possible. I'm delighted to see that at least one of you has already started his work,' as he turned towards Eoin and beamed.

Richie Duffy snorted as the rest of the class stared at Eoin, who blushed.

'Crawler,' hissed Ollie Flanagan.

'All right, enough of that,' said the teacher. 'There's nothing wrong with a bit of enthusiasm for the subject. Now, we've only got five minutes left, so does anyone have any questions?'

'Sir, sir,' said Alan, sticking his hand in the air. 'Do you remember in your first class when you said you might do something about us not having a soccer team in Castlerock? Well, are you going to?'

'We-e-e-ll,' hesitated Mr Lawson, 'I'd have to ask the headmaster about that first. Are many of you interested in football?'

Almost all the hands went up.

'OK, well I don't want it to get too big. Maybe we'll just start it for the guys who don't play rugby. Leave it with me.'

CHAPTER 16

Rory was still in a foul mood over the threat to his place on the first-fifteen. He was still talking to Dylan, but was now blanking Eoin, which perplexed the new captain.

'I don't know what he expects me to say or do,' Eoin complained to Alan on Sunday morning as they lounged around in the dorm. 'I can't pick the team, and Mr McRae has very strong views on what he wants. And Mr Carey has been raving about Dylan every time I've seen him.'

'Just stay out of it, Eoin,' said Alan. 'Rory can be very selfish at times; it's best to let him stew on this till the first team is picked.'

'I know, I know,' said Eoin. 'Anyway, change the subject. Did I tell you what happened when I went over to the library a couple of nights ago?'

'No,' replied Alan.

'I got out that book by Dave Gallaher, the guy who I'm doing the project on. It's an ancient book, but I couldn't believe it when I opened it and saw that it used to be owned by Brian Hanrahan!'

'Who's Brian Hanrahan?' asked Alan.

'Brian. The old player. The ghost,' said Eoin.

'Wow, that's a coincidence. It's more than a coincidence – it's downright spooky.'

'Yeah, but as soon as I opened it, who appeared behind me but Brian himself—'

'You saw a GHOST? In CASTLEROCK?' spluttered Alan.

'Yeah, he didn't stay long because that Mr McDonagh disturbed us. I'm going to see if he'll come back now. Want to come over to the library?'

'Of course!' said Alan. 'Let me get my hoodie.'

The pair jogged over to the library and Eoin asked the librarian for the rugby book.

They wandered down to the back of the room, trying not to look too obviously suspicious. Eoin laid the book on the table and opened it at the title page.

'That's amazing,' said Alan. 'Now how do you make him appear?'

'I dunno.' said Eoin, 'He just did, last time.'

'Maybe he won't appear because I'm here?'

'Well, he did say that he had never been seen by anyone in over eighty years, so maybe there's something about me that means I can see him. But only when I'm on my own.'

'But what about the final?' asked Alan. 'There were thousands there that day and you were still able to see him?'

'I don't know,' said Eoin. 'I don't make up the rules of this.'

They tried shaking the book, or rubbing it, but still there was no sign of Brian. Eoin shrugged his shoulders and headed back to the counter.

'Ah, thank you for that, young man. Will you be needing it again?' asked the librarian.

'I will,' replied Eoin. 'I have to do a project on the writer for the Young Historian Competition.'

'Hmmmm,' said the librarian. 'I have to go away for a few weeks, and I'm not sure how often the library will be open in my absence as it relies on voluntary work. But you have been very careful with this book and I'm sure you will continue to do so. I will sign it out to you for the term of my absence – no one has looked at it in decades so I'm there won't be too many complaints,' he grinned.

Eoin and Alan wandered back to the dormitory, where Rory lay moping on his bed with his earbuds in. They gave him a nod, which he barely returned.

Right behind them, Dylan bounced into the room, looking very happy with himself.

'Howya, lads,' he roared. 'All looking good for the game next week? When's the team getting picked?'

Rory took the buds from his ear and stood up. 'It will be out soon enough. They'll pin it on the noticeboard downstairs. And maybe you could get someone educated to read it out for you, you Limerick skanger—'

With that, Dylan leapt across the room like an angry wolf. He grabbed Rory by the throat and roared in his face.

'Who's a skanger, who's a skanger?' he yelled.

Eoin pulled at Dylan's shoulder. 'Get off him, Dylan, NOW!'

Dylan turned and sneered at Eoin.

'You're all the same when you're up here, Madden, aren't you. No time for the boys from back home, eh?'

Dylan let go of Rory, and turned to walk away. 'Don't EVER call me that again, Grehan, or I'll rip you to pieces. And you know I can.'

As soon as Dylan left, Rory lay down on his bed,

plugged his music into his ears and turned away from his friends.

CHAPTER 17

Eoin was annoyed after the row in the dormitory, so he decided to make his escape. He grabbed *The Complete Rugby Footballer* from his locker, and left without a word.

He was angry with both of his friends, but knew that his position as captain meant he had to stay out of their conflict.

He growled at a junior-school boy who got in his way as he walked out the door, and broke into a trot as he headed for the furthest, quietest corner of the school grounds. It was here, on the banks of a bubbling stream, that he had found the herb that helped him recover from injury before the final last season.

Eoin sat down on a rock and opened up the book, scanning a paragraph or two before he realised he wasn't taking in anything that he had read. He needed to relax. He closed his eyes, just letting the sounds of the water wash over him on the mild autumn day. His peace was soon interrupted by a strange voice.

'Hello, son, I think I recognise that book you're reading. Where did you ever get that old thing?' asked a man who was standing on the other bank of the tiny stream.

Eoin looked closely at the man, who had a thick black moustache and seemed to be wearing a heavy woollen uniform.

'It was in the school library. I'm doing a project on one of the authors,' he explained.

'Well, that's very amusing.' the man replied, 'And is it Billy Stead you're doing your pro-ject on?'

'Eh, no, it's the other one, Dave Gallaher,' said Eoin, 'Why do you ask?'

'Because, little fella, standing here in front of you is Company Sergeant-Major David Gallaher of the Twenty-Second Reinforcements – reporting for duty.'

Eoin stared, not quite sure what to say next. He already suspected he had some sort of ghost-seeing power, and wasn't as rattled by this apparition as he would have been a year earlier.

'I thought you looked a bit familiar,' he started. 'Are you *really* Dave Gallaher?'

'Well I used to be,' the stranger replied. 'I suppose I'm what you'd call a ghost now … Where exactly am I? Your accent is familiar, but you're definitely not from Belgium.'

'No, you're in Ireland. This is a boarding school called Castlerock College. It's in Dublin.'

'Ireland? Wow, that's a long way from Ponsonby. I was born in Donegal, you know, a little place called Ramelton. Don't remember it at all, I'm afraid. I remember the long journey to New Zealand, but nothing of my time in old Ireland. My mother left my baby brother behind, you know. He was ailing and she knew he wouldn't survive the voyage. He died about a year later I think. My poor mother was brokenhearted when she got that letter.'

Eoin stared as the spectre sat down on another boulder on the far side of the stream.

'How did you end up here?' Eoin asked.

'Who knows,' said Dave. 'I've had a very contented existence since a German shell blew me into eternity back in '17. I wandered the former battlefields of Europe for a while, meeting too many old buddies, and I've popped up here and there at rugby grounds when I got a hankering after the great game. But this is the first time I've been back in Ireland. It doesn't seem to have changed that much …'

'Well, you haven't really seen an awful lot of it here hiding in the woods in the corner of the school grounds. You won't recognise much, I'd say,' said Eoin.

'Do they still play rugby here?' the former All Black asked. 'I came over here with the New Zealanders in 1905, 1906, but I had an injured leg and missed the test match. One of my ambitions was to play in my native land, but I was crook so it never happened. I spent most of my time here in bed in the hotel; very disappointed, I was.

'They played in a place called Lansdowne Road if I remember. Is that still there?'

'Well, we certainly *do* play rugby,' explained Eoin. 'The old ground was knocked down a few years ago and they rebuilt it as a brand new stadium. You wouldn't recognise much of it except the grassy bit. But there's a photo of your team on the wall there.'

'Really? Well, isn't that grand. I thought they'd have long forgotten the likes of old Dave Gallaher and Billy Stead. So what's this about a pro-ject?'

Eoin explained what he was planning to write about for the Young Historian Competition, and as he talked an idea came into his head.

'I have this book which covers the rugby, and there's a

load of stuff about you on the internet – eh, I'll explain what that is later – but I can't find much about your time fighting in the war, and that's what the teacher wants it to be about. Would you be able to help me with that?'

'Sounds fair,' said Dave. 'I think I'll hang around here for a while. I like the look of Dublin and I see you play a bit of rugby here too. Maybe I could get some work as a trainer?' He winked at Eoin.

CHAPTER 18

Eoin's head was starting to hurt as he walked back to the dorm. His attempts to escape the bickering had only given him something even more complicated to think about. It was really nice that Dave had agreed to help him with his project – but why on earth had he suddenly become a magnet for dead rugby players?

'Are you OK, Eoin?' asked Alan. 'You look as though you've seen a gho— Oh, sorry, that's the wrong thing to say to YOU!' he joked.

'Well, actually, I have,' whispered Eoin. 'And a new one, too.'

'You're joking, aren't you?' replied Alan, careful to make sure that Rory didn't hear. He still had his earphones in and looked as if he had fallen asleep.

'No,' said Eoin. 'But I don't want to talk about it. This

is all getting too weird.'

He lay down on his bed and closed his eyes. He would have to talk to Mr McRae tomorrow to see who he was thinking of going with at scrum-half. He had been shocked by Dylan's attack on Rory and how it had showed a new side to his fellow Ormondstown boy. That sort of temper could be dangerous.

After history class the next day, Mr Lawson called him back for a word.

'I hear you've been doing some serious research on Dave Gallaher,' he said. 'Mr McDonagh was telling me you tracked down his book on rugby.'

'Yes, sir,' replied Eoin,. 'It's very interesting, although it is only really about rugby. I'm struggling to find information on what he did in the war and all that.

'OK, well I can help you a bit with that,' said Mr Lawson. 'I know a few good New Zealand websites that will steer you in the right direction.'

A knock came to the door, and Mr McRae popped his head in.

'Good morning, Mr Lawson, and Mr Madden, too. How's your All Black research going?' he asked.

'It's going OK, sir,' Eoin replied. 'He was a very interesting man – and I found out why he wasn't in that photo in the Aviva too.'

'Really? That's good work. And why was that?'

'He was crook, and never got to play in either of the games in his native land.'

'Crook,' grinned Mr McRae. 'That's a very Kiwi word, where did you pick that up?'

'Dave told me himself,' blurted Eoin, before he realised what he had said. 'I mean, I mean ... I read it in his book.'

The New Zealanders looked at each other, puzzled, then back at Eoin.

'Eh, OK, Madden, keep up the work and let me know when you need a steer,' said Mr Lawson. 'Did you want a word, Mr McRae?'

'No, Greg, it's actually young Madden I need to talk to,' replied the coach. 'Team business ...' he said, with a wink at the pupil.

As Mr Lawson left for the staffroom for his break, Mr McRae took Eoin out to the rugby field.

'I'm pretty settled on the team for the first game next week,' he started, 'but I'm still torn on the scrum-half. Rory fits in well, and is definitely the better team player, but Dylan has a lot more flair and has a great pair of hands. I think he could really give us an extra dimension, especially because I want you to play at first five-eighth.'

'What's that, sir?' asked Eoin.

'First five-eighth? Oh, I keep forgetting you guys are still in the rugby Stone Age! You know – you call it 'out half'. I want you to wear the No. 10 shirt and I'm going to put Richie Duffy back to No. 12,' explained the coach. 'I've watched the cup final video three times now, and the team got a huge lift when you switched in there when Duffy was injured. What do you think?'

Eoin looked at his feet for a couple of seconds, before raising his gaze to meet that of the coach.

'You're probably right,' he said, 'but Duffy won't be happy and he'll make my life hell. To be honest I haven't had much experience at No. 10. But I'll be fine.

'I really don't know what you should do about No. 9,' he went on. 'Dylan is pushing really hard for it and it's already getting a bit messy – and the two of them are in the same dorm as me.'

'Oooof, that can't be good,' said Mr McRae. 'Try and keep a lid on it, but I'll have to make a call before training tomorrow.'

CHAPTER 19

Eoin desperately wanted to avoid Dylan and Rory, but it was always going to prove impossible when sharing a classroom and a bedroom with both. It was Dylan who approached him first, just as school was ending for the day.

'Look, Eoin,' he started, 'I know Rory's a friend of yours, but you *know* I'm a far better scrum-half than he'll ever be. Can you put a word in with McRae for me?'

'Hang on a minute, Dylan,' said Eoin. 'First of all, I'm not putting a word in with Mr McRae for anyone. I'll make suggestions on what I see and I'm still not convinced about which of you should be in. Rory's a solid scrum-half and he knows the way we play. You're a good player, I agree, but flying off the handle like you did last night doesn't exactly prove you're the man for the job. What were you thinking?'

'Aw, that?' grinned Dylan. 'I was just messing with him. And anyway he started it – calling me a "Limerick skanger" is way out of line – I'm not even *from* Limerick anyway!'

'I agree he was out of order,' said Eoin, 'but flipping out like that was a bit scary. You do that on the pitch and you could lose us the game – and you'd never be picked for the As again.'

'Oh,' said Dylan, 'Is that why you won't put a word in? Just because I lost it with Rory?'

'NO!' replied Eoin, exasperated. 'I'm not putting a word in for EITHER of you. Can't you get that into your head?'

'Fair enough, boss,' Dylan answered, 'but you know it would be a terrible mistake to go with Rory, don't you?' he said as he walked off.

Eoin opened his mouth to reply, but decided against it. He hung his head, completely fed up with the situation in which he had found himself.

He decided to escape from it all in his favourite quiet corner, although he muttered to himself on the way that he hoped the Gallaher ghost wasn't there to disturb him.

He got his wish, because there was no sign of the

long-dead New Zealander, but his wish for peace was disrupted by his other friend from the spirit world.

'Well, Eoin, what's happening this year? You've been very quiet. I presume all is well?' said Brian.

'Ah, Brian, if only it was,' he replied. 'I've had a nightmare few weeks. Well, "nightmare" is probably too strong a word for it compared to what you went through, but I'm fairly fed up with it, all the same.'

Eoin explained the woes that had gathered around his shoulders since being made captain of the first-fifteen.

'Anyway, enough of all that, something very weird happened yesterday right in this very spot. I was reading that book you used to own when suddenly this ghost appeared and said he was Dave Gallaher – the fella who wrote the book!'

'Really? That's very odd indeed. I heard a lot about Gallaher around the club at the time. He was a highly-respected figure. What did he say to you?'

'He told me about his career and how he came to Dublin – and that he was going to stay around Dublin for a while,' replied Eoin. 'I think it was opening the book that brought him here to me. It's obviously got something powerful going on inside. Especially seeing as I have some form in this sort of thing.'

'I suppose it was a very important book to me too,'

said Brian. 'Charlie gave it to me that last Christmas, but it wasn't new. It was already twenty years old. He told me that it had belonged to our father, who died when I was very small. We didn't have very much to remember him by, and I used to think about him every time I opened it.'

'I better be careful with it,' said Eoin. 'I have to get that project moving soon. Any suggestions?'

Brian laughed. 'Sorry, laddie, there's no substitute for doing the work on something like that. And anyway, I wasn't much up for the books myself.'

'The new coach moved me to out-half too,' explained Eoin. 'Which means Richie Duffy will be gunning for me.'

Brian laughed again. 'Well now, Eoin, you're doing a lot of complaining. Just get on with it and everything will be fine. If you HADN'T been moved to out-half you'd be whingeing too,' he added. 'Time to get down to work on your rugby – and your project. I'll drop by to see you soon enough.'

CHAPTER 20

After homework and a comedy show on TV, Eoin slipped away quietly from the common room and climbed the stairs to the dormitory. He didn't want to talk to anyone and was eager to catch up on his sleep.

As he crept through the door he heard someone whispering loudly. There was no one to be seen, but the large lump under the duvet on Dylan's bed gave him away. He was having a telephone conversation with someone.

'Look, Mam, I'm fine. I'll keep a good eye out and I'm sure the headmaster will too. You've nothing to worry about,' Dylan whispered. 'Just make sure you're OK yourself.'

Eoin stopped, sensing it wasn't the sort of conversation he needed to hear. He backed out of the room and down the corridor, before re-entering the room singing loudly.

'Hi guys! Anyone home?' he called out, walking into the room. Dylan didn't budge, but he had stopped talking. Eoin didn't hear another peep out of him, so he too slipped into bed and turned off the lights.

Next afternoon, the A squad assembled for training. There was a distinct atmosphere of nervousness in the changing room, and Eoin wasn't too happy to see that Dylan was now sitting in the corner alongside Duffy and his hangers-on.

In walked Mr McRae, carrying a clipboard and wearing a whistle on a lanyard around his neck.

'Right, mateys, let's settle down,' the coach started. 'I've spent good bit of time assessing your skills and commitment, and I'm impressed. I've also been looking at the video of the final last year, and it's on that basis that I've made my selection for the first game of the season on Saturday. Personnel wise, I'm not making any changes, but I am going to make a switch in the backs, with Madden and Duffy changing places at 12 and 10.'

Eoin decided it was best not to look around this time, so he continued to stare at the coach's whistle.

'As you know, I've also asked Eoin to skipper the team, but I want you *all* to take responsibility for your play, and to help out your team-mates at all times. This is a team game and the best teams are those that battle alongside each other out on the paddock. Any questions?'

Nobody moved, but a few stole sidewards glances at Richie Duffy. Eventually the ousted out-half piped up.

'Is that for the whole season or just this first game?' he asked.

'Well ...' said Mr McRae, 'I'd prefer to think that you can all focus on the position you're going to play from now on. I'll be flexible if I need to be, but it would take something major for me to make changes. I think you're a good footballer, Duffy, but the team definitely upped their game when Madden slotted in at first five-eighth in that final. I think he brings something extra at No. 10, and you have the skills to do a good job at No. 12.'

Duffy grunted in reply, before standing up and starting to head for the door.

'Mr Duffy, I'll tell you to leave when I am ready. Now sit back there and listen to what I have to say. I want to go through what I want to do at training today.'

Duffy stopped, and with another grunt he sat back down until the coach was finished and the whole squad were sent outside to the rugby field.

Rory came up behind him and slapped Eoin's back. 'Thanks, skipper,' he said, 'Good decision'.

Dylan, who was just in front trotting alongside Richie,

turned and glowered at Rory, before Eoin put up his hand.

'Stop it, you two, NOW!' he shouted. 'I consider both of you my friends – for the moment anyway – and I've had *nothing* to do with the selection of that team. But for the record, I don't have a problem with Mr McRae's call, and I suggest the two of you get on with it and work to prove him right – or wrong.'

He turned and jogged away to his position and waited for training to begin. 'What a pair of babies they are,' he muttered. 'And I'm the unpaid babysitter.'

CHAPTER 21

Eoin realised that telling the rival scrum-halves where to get off was the right thing to have done, so he didn't bother tiptoeing around them after that. There was too much to do, what with being team captain and having daily chats with Mr McRae about tactics, as well as training, study and homework. And then there was the project!

Eoin had let the project slide for a while now, although he had finally managed to work his way through *The Complete Rugby Footballer*. He had found out some details about Dave Gallaher's sporting career, and about his life in New Zealand, but he needed more information about what it was like to fight on the Western Front.

He picked up the ancient book from his locker,

collected a notebook and pen, and wandered out of the school toward his secret haunt. On the way, he bumped into Mr Finn, who was his usual enthusiastic self and was even more so when he saw what Eoin was carrying.

'It's for a history project,' Eoin explained.

'Excellent – is that for the Young Historian competition?' asked the teacher.

'Yes, I'm doing it on Dave Gallaher – I got interested in him when you pointed him out at the Aviva that evening,' he added.

'Wonderful!' said Mr Finn, 'I'm so glad to hear that. You should ask Dixie about him too. I'm sure we discussed him many years ago.'

'I will, thanks,' said Eoin, itching to escape to his hideaway. 'As it's a nice evening I'm just going over to find a quiet corner to read the book.'

Mr Finn bade him goodbye and Eoin broke into a trot towards the tiny stream in the woods.

He sat on the rock and opened the book. Almost immediately Dave appeared.

'Hello there, young laddie, and how have you been?' he asked.

Eoin explained that he wanted to hear about his experiences in the First World War and what it was like in the trenches of Flanders.

'It wasn't pretty, I'll tell you that,' Dave Gallaher started, 'I had been a soldier a long time before in South Africa, when we fought the Boers. I was well into my forties when the Great War started. Two of my little brothers, Charlie and Douglas, went off to fight, and to be honest I wanted to go too. Lots of rugby mates signed up, and when the newspapers started reporting their deaths I felt a terrible tug. But I was married to Nellie, and had a lovely little girl called Nora, so …' he paused, staring at his feet.

'But both my brothers were badly injured in Gallipoli so I decided to sign up so that the Gallahers could continue to play their part. Douglas went back to the Western Front and I applied to rejoin the army. I was waiting for the call-up when my mother got that awful telegram saying Douglas had been killed at The Somme.

'They made me a Sergeant-Major and we sailed for Europe on a big steam ship – it took us three months to get here, would you believe? – and eventually we were sent to the front line in Belgium. I think it was spelled "Ypres", but everyone called it "Wipers".

'We were fighting over a town called Passchendaele, but to be honest there wasn't much to fight for. Every single building had been levelled and the whole area was just one big bomb site of churned-up mud and slime. I think I heard that more than half a million men died in that small area and, of course, I was one of them …'

Dave sat down on the rock beside Eoin, and the schoolboy could feel a chill in the air.

'It's hard to talk about it even now, but you're a bright kid, and I suppose it could do some good if it helps people understand how horrible war can be.

'The terrible thing was how young they all were. I was a grown man, nearly forty-four, but everyone in my company was half my age or younger. Some of them were younger than the senior boys in your school I saw playing rugby yesterday. I even met a few lads from rugby clubs who had joined up together as if it was some exciting away game they were going to.

'I didn't see much action, as I was mortally wounded on the second day of fighting, but I still saw some terrible sights.'

Dave went on to tell Eoin the grim story of his last day on the battlefield, and about all the friends he saw die in the misery of the trenches.

'And all those young lads, every one of them cried out for their mother as they died,' he sighed.

By the time he had finished, his ghostly eyes were wet and rimmed with red. Eoin, too, fought with his emotions.

'Have you enough there, son?' asked the Anzac hero.

'I think so, thank you very much for telling me all about it. It's a very sad story,' replied Eoin.

'It is indeed, and I don't think anyone learned from our sacrifice either,' he added, with a grimace. 'Since then, the world seems to have been full of war and misery ...'

CHAPTER 22

Castlerock won their first four games of the season quite easily, and Mr McRae's hunch about switching Eoin and Richie proved to be a stroke of genius. Both players upped their game and already Mr McCaffrey was licking his lips about some more silverware heading for his trophy cabinet.

'I've been very impressed with your tactical kicking, Eoin,' the headmaster told him one day in the playground. 'You are blessed with a fine right foot, but even more importantly you seem to know just when a kick is what is needed. Keep working at it and you will become a very good rugby player indeed,' he beamed.

Eoin, who never knew how to accept praise, felt himself turning pink, especially when Rory and Alan came up alongside.

'I was just telling Madden here that he has a splendid knack as a kicking out-half, as well as off the ground,' said Mr McCaffrey. 'But that's enough about rugby; how are your projects coming along gentlemen?'

The boys all muttered 'fine', but the headmaster pressed Eoin further.

'I'm fascinated by your choice of subject – something like that could well appeal to the judges in the competition. I do hope you all work at your projects as it could bring enormous glory on yourselves, as well as the school. And of course that marvellous prize ...'

Mr McCaffrey was called away and the boys sighed in relief.

'You don't seem to be able to do anything wrong at the moment, Eoin,' grinned Rory. '*A foss-inating choice of sob-ject,*' he chuckled, impersonating the headmaster.

'Leave it out, Rory, it's not my fault he finds my project so excellent,' sniggered Eoin. 'It's certainly better than "Road signs of South Dublin, 1950-2000", or whatever it is you're doing.'

Rory looked sheepish. 'Ah look, history isn't my subject at all – and I found a deadly website that has done all the work on it.'

'You'd better not get caught,' Alan warned. 'Mr Lawson doesn't seem to be much crack, and if McCaffrey finds out you'll be in serious trouble.'

'Ah sure, I'm only doing it because I have to,' laughed Rory. 'I don't expect to get picked to go to the RDS. I don't want to be spending all my time there stuck at a stand answering boring questions – I want to be around the hall having the crack with the young ladies.'

The boys wandered back to class.

'Is Dylan still blanking you?' Eoin asked Rory.

'Yeah,' he replied. 'But I'm not too worried.'

'Ah, look, he's not a bad lad at all,' said Eoin. 'He's a bit chippy, but he's decent. I hope you can sort it out.'

'It won't be sorted until I break my leg and he gets my No. 9 shirt,' said Rory. 'I'm not bragging, but I'm playing really well this year and there's no doubt the extra competition is the reason why.'

Eoin agreed, and took his seat for Mr Lawson's history class.

The teacher handed Eoin some print-outs about Dave Gallaher and they discussed how his project was going.

'Photographs are important too, and any memorabilia you can lay your hands on,' he told Eoin. 'That's not going to happen easily with a subject from the wrong side of the world and nearly a hundred years dead, but have a look on the internet for some pictures anyway.'

He addressed the whole class. 'Next week is half-term, and I don't expect you to spend *all* your free time working on the project – but I do want to see some progress when we meet again on Monday week. Spend an afternoon or two on it, and you won't be rushing as the deadline approaches.'

As they left the classroom, Eoin caught up with Dylan.

'Hi, Dyl, how are you getting home tonight?' he asked. 'My dad is collecting me and he'll be on his own so there'll be plenty of room. I rang him last night and he said it would be OK.'

Dylan looked at him with darkened eyes.

'I'll be fine, Madden, don't you worry about me,' he snarled.

Eoin backed off. 'OK, I just thought you might be stuck. The bus would be no fun tonight in this weather.'

Dylan turned his back on Eoin and stormed off towards the dormitory.

CHAPTER 23

Eoin's dad was a bit surprised to hear that Dylan wasn't taking a lift home to Ormondstown, but decided to lay off the subject when he saw Eoin's reaction.

On the way down they discussed how the term had gone, and Eoin explained about his history project.

'Gosh, that sounds very interesting. It's funny, I've never been that interested in rugby, but Dave Gallaher is a name I do remember hearing,' said his dad.

'Well Mr Finn said that Grandad knew something about him. I'll have a chat with him over the weekend,' said Eoin.

As they neared Ormondstown, Eoin decided to broach the subject of his classmate once again.

'Dad, have you ever heard anything around town

about Dylan or his family. He's blanked me recently for no reason, and he refused to take a lift tonight. There's something not quite right there – he's not a bad lad at all, but he flies off the handle when he doesn't get his way …'

'I'm not sure, Eoin,' replied his father, 'Families are funny things at times, and I'm not sure Dylan's is the happiest. I'll try to get to the bottom of it, but remember – it isn't something he'd thank you for getting involved in. You should seek him out this week for a kick-about and see what comes of it.'

Eoin's mum was outside the house when the car pulled up. She hugged her son and fussed over him as she helped him carry his bags inside.

'You've lost weight, Eoin. Are you eating properly? I hope you're not training too hard.'

'Ah, Mum, I'm fine,' he shrugged. 'I've never studied as hard as I've done this year. I've even brought my History project home with me for the mid-term break.'

His mother clasped her hands together in delight, before stepping back and looking at him suspiciously.

'Is that some sort of punishment …?'

'NO! I've entered the Young Historian of the Year competition and I'm really enjoying it. And Mr Finn says Grandad might be able to help me with it too.'

His mother beamed at him. 'That's lovely, he'd really enjoy that. He said he would call up this evening – as soon as he heard you were coming home.'

Sure enough, Dixie was delighted to see Eoin, and was full of questions about life at Castlerock College. He had been a very good rugby player in his youth, but had given up the game in tragic circumstances.

'Tell Grandad about your project, Eoin. Didn't you say he might be able to help?' asked his mother.

'Oh yes, of course,' said Eoin.

He explained about the competition, and how he had seen the photo of the old New Zealand team in the Aviva Stadium, and how he hit upon the idea of studying one of their players for the project.

'And which one of the players was that?' quizzed his grandad.

'A man called Dave—'

'—Gallaher!' his grandad completed the name. 'Well isn't that interesting! And yes, I suppose I can help you with that, in a small way.'

'How's that?' asked Eoin. 'He died long before you were born?'

'Well, it wasn't that long,' laughed Dixie, 'maybe twenty-five years or so!'

'No, I obviously never met him or got to see him play,

but I met someone who did meet him. It was an old priest who came to see me after your grandmother died. He was a fair age, and we got talking about rugby. He didn't know much about it, but said he had once met a man who had captained the All Blacks.

'This priest was a chaplain during the First World War and saw some terrible sights in the trenches. He told me that one day he was visiting a field hospital where he was brought into a tent to give the last rites to a group of men who had been badly injured that day.

'He told me he was tending to one poor soul who was clearly close to death when he read his dog tags and realised who the man was. The priest said that he prayed over him to help him on his way, and then moved on to the next wounded soldier. 'Do you know who that is on the next table?' he asked the soldier. 'That's Dave Gallaher, captain of the 1905 All Blacks'. The priest said that he often thought of how sad it was that such an obviously remarkable man had his life cut short by war. He even gave me a copy of a poem that a friend of his, another chaplain, wrote about that very subject. I'll dig it out for you if I can.'

'That's a sad story, Grandad,' said Eoin. 'Can I use it in my project? Do you remember the priest's name?'

'Of course you can use it – I'll try to remember a few

more details – and the priest? Was his name Fitzpatrick? Something like that … Fitz, Fitz, Fitzgerald – that's who it was. Father Edward Fitzgerald.'

CHAPTER 24

Monday morning was wet and miserable in Tipperary, so Eoin decided to get the project work out of the way so he could have a nice break for the rest of the week. He set out all the information he had gleaned, and wrote up his grandad's anecdote about the death of Dave Gallaher. He would need to seek out the old player's ghost again, as he was still missing some parts of his story.

The day went quickly and when the rain cleared away Eoin decided to go out for a run. He jogged down to the GAA club to see if his old pals were around, but the only person to be seen was Barney who was fixing the goal nets.

'How are you, Barney?' hailed Eoin. 'The opposition must have been cracking them in at the weekend if you have to fix those!' he joked.

'Arra, sure, we hammered them. A shower from down the county, wouldn't know much about hurling down there,' the old groundsman replied. 'How are you getting on up in Dublin? I heard you were getting good at the rugby.'

'Ah, where did you hear that Barney?'

'Well now, your grandfather comes down to me nearly every day for a chat. He's very fond of you, you know. He said you remind him of how he used to play the game. He was a bit of a rugby player himself, I think.'

'He was indeed. He could have played for Ireland, they say,' replied Eoin.

'And sure maybe you will some day,' said Barney 'Unless you stick with the football and hurling of course!'

Eoin laughed and jogged away, happy to see one of the characters of his hometown. It was people like Barney that he missed when he was away. The faces and places he took for granted while growing up were precious now he was living in Dublin for most of the year.

He was shaken out of his thoughts as he turned the corner into the main street, because there standing outside the newsagents with two other boys was Dylan.

'Howya, Dyl. Did you get down OK that night?' he asked.

Dylan stopped talking to his pals and turned towards Eoin.

'I was fine. What's it to you?' he replied.

'All right, have it like that if you want,' Eoin came back, 'but you have no argument with me. Give me a shout if you want to sort it out. I'll be down the Gaels in the morning.'

He jogged off up the street, still perplexed as to why Dylan had such a problem with him. He wasn't too impressed with the company he was keeping either. The Moylan brothers were the cause of most of the trouble in Eoin's primary-school class before he left for Dublin.

When Eoin got home, his mum and dad were waiting for him. His dad had a serious face, and Eoin suddenly felt concerned when he sat down.

'What's wrong, is it Grandad?' he asked.

'No, no, nothing like that at all,' his mother said. 'Your dad met one of his fishing pals today and he had some interesting information to tell him.'

'My fishing pal is the local Garda Superintendent during the week,' explained his dad. 'I asked him about Dylan and he was telling me that he has come to their attention recently.'

'Oh, no,' said Eoin. 'But how? He's been in Dublin since September …'

'He's not in any trouble,' said Mr Madden, 'well not with the Guards anyway. It seems Dylan's father is a "major gangland figure" as they say on the television news. His mother is a good woman, however, and she walked out on him one day and took Dylan and his little sister with her. He has one older brother who has already been in prison and his mother was terrified that Dylan would join him there. Dylan isn't even his real name, and nor is Coonan. They've been moving around, trying to keep one step ahead of the father who is very keen to have him back.

'Now, you must never breathe a word of this to anyone, and certainly don't let on to Dylan that you know,' warned his father. 'But I think it would be the right thing to do to make up with him and try to be his friend. He's had a hard life and he needs good pals.'

Eoin was stunned at this news, which certainly explained some of Dylan's behaviour and that strange phone conversation in the dormitory. He agreed that he would try to sort his differences with Dylan.

CHAPTER 25

Eoin didn't bump into his classmate around town all week; on Friday afternoon he decided to call around to his house. He knew the street Dylan lived on, but didn't know the number, so he called into the newsagent on the corner.

'I'm sorry, do you know where the Coonans live, please?' he asked.

'Why do you ask?' replied the assistant, suspiciously.

'I'm in school with Dylan,' Eoin replied.

'Up in Dublin?' she countered.

'Yeah. I play Gaelic with him as well …'

'OK, you must be Eoin Madden so. They're in number six, two doors down. Knock twice on the window and then on the door,' she told him.

Eoin was a bit surprised at the rigmarole involved in

calling to Dylan, but slowly realised it might have been something to do with what his father had learned.

He did as the shop assistant had said, and the door was opened by a girl a little bit younger than him with red hair. She looked him up and down and asked him his name.

'Eoin Madden,' he replied. 'I'm in school with Dylan.'

'Ah, I've heard a bit about you. He's upstairs on the computer. I'm Caoimhe.'

She called up to her brother, and shrugged her shoulders when he grunted his reply.

'Have you any sisters?' Caoimhe asked Eoin.

Eoin was a bit taken aback. 'Eh, no,' he spluttered. 'No brothers either.'

'I was just wondering,' she replied. 'I know nearly all the girls in the convent school and there's none called Madden.'

'How do you like the school?' he asked.

'Ah, it's all right,' Caoimhe replied. 'I'd talk to anyone, but some of them are a bit snooty. There's a good library there though. I prefer books to kids most of the time.'

They chatted for a couple of minutes more before Dylan finally came down stairs.

'All right, Eoin, what's up?' he asked.

'Howya, Dylan, you want to go for a run?' asked Eoin.

'Nah, I'm busy,' said Dylan.

A woman came into the hallway. 'Come on now, Dyl, you've been up there for hours. A bit of air will do you good. I need milk and bread, too.'

She handed Dylan a five euro note and held open the front door. 'OK, Mum,' he growled.

The boys wandered down the street silently, before Eoin eventually broke the ice.

'Look, Dyl, I had nothing to do with you not being picked, but you can choose not to believe that if you want. I'm not your enemy, and I even thought I was your friend. That school can be a rough place for a new boy – I had a few problems myself there last year – but it's a lot easier if you're hanging around with a good bunch of lads.'

'I am,' said Dylan. 'Richie and his crew are decent enough.'

'Yeah, well, I didn't see much of that myself, but even so it's pointless to keep blanking the rest of us in the dorm.'

Dylan stayed silent for another minute, before he stopped and turned to look at Eoin.

'OK, I've been a bit of a brat, I suppose, but it's hard to fit in there,' Dylan started. 'You're such a legend already in Castlerock. I know I'm a good scrum-half – and I'm probably better than Rory – but because I'm new I have to be twice as good as everyone else to get a look in.'

Eoin nodded. 'I know, and I had a bit of that myself last year. But acting like a spoilt brat only reduces your chances of getting in. You need to work at it, maybe even switch positions – there might be a slot on the wing now Shane has a dodgy ankle.'

'Do you reckon?' asked Dylan. 'Would McRae allow me to switch to the wing?'

'Well, on the Bs to start with, I suppose,' suggested Eoin. 'But you have the pace and you're a tough one when you need to be. I think you'd make a cracking wing.' Eoin put his arm on Dylan's shoulder. 'Look, let's start this year off again on a better foot. I don't have any other Ormondstown Gaels with me up in Dublin, so I'm relying on you to be my buddy. You know I don't get on with Richie, but fair play to you if you do. I'm not going to say anything to put you off him, but just be careful there.'

'Ah, I know,' replied Dylan, 'He was decent enough when I was fighting with you, but I suspect he won't want to know me now we're mates again.'

CHAPTER 26

They had a good kick-about that day in the Gaels, with Eoin suggesting a few moves that Dylan might add to his game to make him a potential Castlerock winger. By the end of the day they were laughing and joking like best buddies.

Dylan was happy to take a lift back to Dublin too, and it was a happy, pleasant group that pulled up the drive to Castlerock College at the end of the mid-term break.

'Thanks, Mr Madden,' said Dylan as the boys took their bags out of the boot of his car.

Eoin hung back to thank his dad.

'I'm glad to see things have worked out better,' said Dad. 'He's a nice young fella, just needs a bit of stability in his life, I'd reckon.'

'Cheers, Dad. I'll keep in touch,' said Eoin. 'And try to

reply to my texts!'

'I will, I will,' laughed his dad, 'You young lads don't know how busy life is for parents. I don't have time to be composing texts. And to be honest, I'm not entirely sure how this new phone works either ...'

Eoin chuckled to himself as he climbed the stairs to the dormitory.

As he turned the corner he bumped into Dylan, who was talking to Mr McCaffrey. It was a serious conversation.

'Sorry. I didn't see you,' Eoin apologised.

Dylan shrugged and looked at Eoin, but didn't say a word. Eoin went into the dorm and shut the door. Alan bounced up from the bed, where he was reading a zombie comic.

'Howya, Eoin, have a good break?' he asked.

'Yeah, not bad at all. Got a bit of work done. You?'

'Boring. Rained a lot. Tried to start work on my project about Ancient Greece, but there always seemed to be something more interesting on TV. I watched a documentary about goats at one stage.'

'Ha! Ancient Greek goats I hope? I'm pretty much done on the research for my thing so I'll get down to writing it this week.'

Dylan walked in just then, but besides the usual

'hellos' he was obviously not in the mood for a chat and lay down on his bed and plugged in his earphones. Eoin noticed the music player wasn't even switched on.

Dylan just didn't want to talk.

Although he was friendly enough, Dylan still hadn't had anything more than a basic conversation with any of his schoolmates by Wednesday afternoon, when the Under-14s lined out for their first league game.

By coincidence, the match was against St Osgur's, the team they had beaten in the final at the Aviva at the end of the previous season.

'I'm sure these guys will be stoked about this game.' said Mr McRae, 'And from what I saw of them in the final they're a nifty side. But if you stick to the basics she'll be right. You all know your role and your respon-sibilities. So go out there and show them that the final was no flash in the pan – Castlerock are the best team in the province at this age group, and those guys better remember that.'

The team cheered as the coach's stirring words echoed around the dressing room. It was their first chance to play in the school since the Aviva, too, and there was a big turnout of boys from the older classes.

It was clear from early on that St Osgur's hadn't forgotten the final and were keen to hand out some revenge. Richie Duffy didn't help, either, singing 'cham-pion-es, cham-pion-es' as the ball was put into the first scrum of the game. The referee stopped play and walked over to Eoin.

'Ask your opera singer to keep it zipped, please, captain,' he snapped.

St Osgur's steamed upfield and were 6-0 up within ten minutes as Castlerock, defending desperately, kept conceding penalties. The first time Duffy got the ball he foolishly tried a sidestep and run, but the visitors were only waiting for such an opportunity and he was flattened by three large forwards coming at him from left, right and centre.

The three rose to their feet sporting huge grins as their team-mates started singing 'Always Look On The Bright Side Of Life' before the referee waved his finger at them.

Richie was battered and bruised, but after a couple of minutes he was ready to resume his position. While many of the Castlerock boys weren't too fond of Duffy, and even understood why the St Osgur's players had done it – Richie was a member of THEIR team and he needed to be protected, and avenged.

The Castlerock pack won a series of scrums and rucks

which took them into the opposition 22 when Rory fired the ball out to Eoin at out-half. Eoin spotted a gap and went for it, and with a sharp injection of pace he burst through the flailing hands of the St Osgur's defence. In half a second he was clear, and touched the ball down between the posts. He took the congratulations of his team-mates before ushering them back to half-way. He took the conversion himself, and for a second he thought he was back among the blackberry bushes of Ormondstown. Just as he did all summer in the GAA grounds, his kick split the air between the goalposts, and Castlerock were 7-6 in front.

At half-time Mr McRae was positive about their performance, but he took Eoin aside for a private chat just before the second half kicked off.

'Duffy still looks a bit groggy. I'll give him five minutes and then I'll take him off. I was thinking about moving Mikey O'Reilly into centre but that leaves us short of a winger. What do you think?' the coach asked.

'Dylan is keen to play on the wing, and he's definitely got more speed than Joseph,' replied Eoin. 'He won't let you down.'

Mr McRae nodded, but did not reply. He looked over at the bench where the replacements were huddled.

Dylan was nowhere to be seen.

'Mr McCaffrey took him away during the first half. Something's up at home I think.'

CHAPTER 27

Richie Duffy recovered his verve in the second half, and Mr McRae left him on the field. In fact, he scored two of Castlerock's four tries as the home team sauntered to a 28-16 win. Eoin led the cheers for St Osgur's as the teams walked off, and again looked over towards the substitutes. Dylan hadn't returned.

After dinner, Eoin returned to the dormitory, by now very concerned about his friend. He found him lying on his bed, and it was obvious he had been crying.

'Hi, Dyl, what happened today?' Eoin asked. 'Mr McRae was about to bring you on as winger.'

Dylan didn't reply, but sat up and walked over to the door, checked the corridor outside and closed the door behind him. He walked back to his bed, sat down and looked up at his friend.

'OK, Eoin, what I'm going to tell you HAS to stay between us. You can't tell anyone at all. *Anyone.* Do you promise?'

Eoin nodded.

'It's about my dad. He's not a very nice man, to be honest. I haven't seen him since I was little, and most of my memories are of him being mean to my mother. Mum took Caoimhe and me away a good while ago, but he was, eh, away for a while so he didn't bother us.

'We were in Limerick for a few years but Mum got nervous there and so we moved to Ormondstown. We really like it there and she has a nice job too,' he said.

'One of her uncles was a rich lawyer in America and he wanted me to come to school here so he's paying the fees. He was in Castlerock with Mr McCaffrey and explained the situation to him – and asked him to keep an eye out for me.

'McCaffrey got a call from Mum today saying she had seen one of my dad's cronies around Ormondstown. She doesn't think he saw her, but she's terrified all the same. It's funny, she was nervous last week but I told her not to worry. Mothers always have an instinct about these things …'

Eoin sat down on the bed opposite Dylan.

'That's shocking, Dyl,' he started. 'Is she OK? Why did

you have to leave the game?'

'She's fine now, but she doesn't know anyone well enough to trust in Ormondstown so she's not leaving the house and poor old Caoimhe's staying home from school. McCaffrey brought me over to talk to her as she was very upset when she rang him. Caoimhe's in a state too, but she's tougher than you think ...'

Dylan blinked hard and changed the subject. 'Was McRae going to bring me on? Really?'

'Yeah, he was going to switch the backs around a bit when Richie got injured. I told him you were a better bet on the wing than Joseph,' said Eoin.

'Thanks, buddy,' said Dylan, suddenly cheered up. 'I'll make sure I'm up for it at training on Friday.'

The pair wandered down to the common-room where Chelsea were getting a hammering from Barcelona on TV. Eoin chuckled to himself as blues fan Richie Duffy sat grey-faced in front of the screen.

Eoin sat down in a quiet corner and took out *The Complete Rugby Footballer* and the notes for his project. He had lots of good information and a few ideas for how he would approach the project, but he was missing the magic that would give it a chance of winning. He would need to see Dave again soon.

CHAPTER 28

The next week was spent writing up the project, and Mr Lawson was very pleased with the way Eoin had put it together. He even called Mr Finn into the classroom to read the first draft.

'That's a lovely bit of work, Eoin, and some marvellous stories too. How did you come up with that yarn about the priest?' he asked.

'My grandfather,' replied Eoin. 'He met him a long time ago, just after, just after ...'

'Ah, yes of course. I remember. He had been a chaplain in the First World War. Dixie told me the story at the time. It made a great impression on him I recall. And it is interesting that his grandson should have picked up that relay baton, so to speak!'

Eoin smiled, and returned to his work. The deadline

for entries was two days away, and he wasn't happy with some parts of the project. Mr Lawson had come up with a couple of great pictures off the internet, and the librarian had allowed him to photocopy parts of *The Complete Rugby Footballer*, but he wouldn't allow him to send the valuable old book into the competition. So there was nothing connected to Dave Gallaher from his time that would give the project an edge over the other entries.

After school he packed his bag and sauntered over to the stream where he had previously encountered Gallaher. He sat down on the rock and opened the book. It was already starting to get dark, and the evening was starting to get chilly. He wouldn't be able to hang around too long.

He stared at the photograph of Gallaher and his teammate and co-author Billy Stead. The former rugby captain looked so strong and fit. It was hard to believe that anything could have stopped a man like him, but then he remembered how lethal were the weapons that humans were able to turn on each other, and how it took an eighteen-pound shell packed with high explosive to finally take the life of Segeant-Major David Gallaher of Ramelton and Auckland.

'How are you, lad,' came a voice in the now familiar

Kiwi accent. 'And how's that pro-ject you're working on?'

'Hi, Dave,' said Eoin, relieved that the ghost had shown up. 'It's nearly finished, actually. I just need a couple more questions answered, if you don't mind.'

Dave was able to fill Eoin in on what he needed to know, and they chatted for a while about the modern world of rugby and how very different a sport it appeared to the old All Black.

'I watched a bit of that game you played last week. You guys are pretty slick. But I couldn't work out half the positions you play in – in my day the half backs were in charge of the left or right side of the field, and who-ever's area it was in put the ball into the scrum, with the other standing off him. You seem to have one little guy to do that all the time now, and of course you played as the stand-off.'

Eoin was relatively new to rugby, but explained it as best he could and hoped he hadn't given Dave a wrong steer. He told him when their next home game was and suggested he come along.

As Eoin rose to leave, he remembered that his pro-ject was still missing any sort of historical artefacts. He explained his problem to Dave.

'Well now, I can probably help you there, son, but

you're going to have to promise to look after them for me. They mean more than life itself to me now, and I've got all eternity to look at them.'

The old soldier opened the breast pocket of his tunic, and took out two items.

'This here's a photo of my wife, Nellie. She's sitting with my lovely daughter Nora. She was just nine years old when I headed off to Europe.'

He handed the faded, browning piece of stiff card to Eoin, and his eyes misted over. 'Look after it good,' he croaked.

And then he opened his fist, which had been closed over a piece of dark cloth.

'This here has been in my pocket for more than a century. I carried it everywhere after I stopped playing, and it went with me to that last battlefield near Wipers.'

Eoin stared at the treasured piece of material, with a silver fern carefully embroidered on the black cloth.

'Before it ended up in my pocket I wore it on my chest, on the black jersey of New Zealand,' the All Black explained. 'Good luck with the pro-ject, I'm chuffed that people will be hearing about Dave Gallaher all over again – and in Ireland too. Drop back here and let me know how it goes.'

CHAPTER 29

Next morning there was another surprise for Eoin, as the school secretary met him on the steps of the school and handed him a letter. The address was written in thin, shaky handwriting, but Eoin recognised the postmark as coming from Ormondstown.

'Grandad,' he smiled. 'And what have you got for me here?'

He opened the letter carefully, and was astonished to find there was just one, yellow piece of paper inside. It was clearly very old, and when he opened it, a poem was printed on it in very old-fashioned script. He read it to himself.

Waste of muscle, waste of brain
Waste of patience, waste of pain
Waste of manhood, waste of health

Waste of beauty, waste of wealth
Waste of blood and waste of tears
Waste of youth's most precious years
Waste of ways the Saints have trod
Waste of glory
Waste of God
War!

Underneath the poem was written a note in different handwriting.

'Poem hand-written by the author, Geoffrey Studdert Kennedy, and given by him to Father Edward Fitzgerald, the man who gave the last rites to Dave Gallaher.'

Eoin grinned, and kissed the envelope. 'Thanks, Grandad,' he said to himself. 'That's fantastic.'

Mr Lawson was stunned when Eoin produced the folder containing his final project, which he had coloured to resemble Dave's old book, and he was knocked out by the three pieces of history that he produced to accompany his entry.

'Where on earth did you get these items?' he asked.

Eoin panicked, realising he couldn't tell the whole truth without getting into a whole lot more trouble. But he couldn't tell a lie to the teacher either.

'My grandad gave me the poem,' he replied. 'He met the old priest, Fr Fitzgerald, a long time ago. It was just a coincidence that I told him I was doing the project on Dave Gallaher.'

'And the photograph? I gave you a print-out of that from a website. But this looks like the original ...'

'A friend of mine gave it to me,' Eoin explained. 'He heard I was doing the project and got it to me. I have to look after it really carefully. Can we just send a copy to the organisers and bring this along to the exhibition? I just can't lose them.'

'And the silver fern,' asked Mr Lawson. 'Is this ...?' he stared at Eoin. 'It *can't* be!'

'It is,' said Eoin. 'The same friend.'

'But, that's a truly priceless artefact. I know for certain that the New Zealand National Museum would pay a fortune for such an item, let alone what private collectors might. I'm not a huge rugby fan, but this gives me the shivers just holding it. Who is this friend?' he asked.

'I would rather not say,' said Eoin. 'Security issues, you know.'

Mr Lawson stared at the youngster. 'Well, I must say I'm seriously impressed, Eoin, this is a brilliant piece of work. No matter how well you do in the competition I'd say you're a certainty for an A in your next school report. Well done.'

CHAPTER 30

The Under-14s won their next two games, and already were being talked of as favourites for the Begley Cup. They had been drawn to play against St Isolde's Academy in the semi-final and there was a real buzz around the school about the team.

Unfortunately, the team suffered a setback just before the big game.

Mr Lawson had asked Mr McCaffrey could he set up a small soccer club, but the headmaster needed a lot of convincing. Castlerock was a rugby school, and nothing could be allowed deflect from its aim to be the best rugby school in the province. The New Zealander pointed out that there were a lot of boys who couldn't get into the three Under-14 rugby teams and were missing out on healthy activity.

Reluctantly, Mr McCaffrey agreed and Castlerock AFC was granted a small, scruffy pitch in a distant corner of the playing fields.

They played among themselves at first, but the trouble came during a friendly against Ligouri College. The team was mostly made up of boys who didn't play rugby, but there was a handful of rugby players on the team. Just before the final whistle one of them, Joseph Pearse, was through on his own with only the goalkeeper to beat when he suddenly lurched forward and tumbled to the ground. He roared in pain, and Mr Lawson rushed out to where he lay.

'What's up, Joseph?'

'Aaaaah, it's agony, sir. I went into a pothole and twisted my ankle and went over. It feels like it's broken sir,' the boy replied.

Happily for Joseph, his ankle wasn't broken, but it was seriously sprained and he was told to rest it for a week. Which meant he would miss the Begley Cup semi-final.

Mr McCaffrey and Mr Carey were furious – and ordered Mr Lawson not to use members of the rugby teams any more – but Mr McRae didn't seem too put out by losing his left winger. He took Eoin aside before the last light training session the following day.

'All right, skipper, here's what I'm thinking,' the coach

began. 'I'm going to bring Dylan in on the wing. I've been looking at him a lot in training and I agree that he has great potential there. He is a bit small, I suppose, but he has a great burst of speed and passes well. What do you think?'

Eoin agreed, and took it on himself to tell Dylan. His room-mate's grin was as wide as the Ormondstown Gaels goal.

'Fantastic! Thanks bud,' he replied. 'I won't let you down'.

And Dylan certainly didn't let Eoin or Mr McRae down. The little winger was unstoppable, and every time he received the ball he caused havoc in the St Isolde's defence. He nipped in for a try just before half time to give Castlerock a 13-11 lead, but came into his own in the second half as the forwards' domination started to pay off.

'Get the ball out to the wings as soon as possible,' Eoin told the backs when they came together for a huddle mid-way through the half with the score reading 16-14. 'Shane and Dylan have the legs on them to cause huge damage.'

Eoin proved right, with Dylan running in three more tries as Castlerock strolled into the final. As the referee's last whistle rang out, the scoreboard showed an emphatic

35-14 win for Mr McRae's team. The coach shook all their hands as they reached the dressing room.

'That was a truly splendid display,' he told them. 'I'm dead proud of what you did out there today, which is all down to the work you've been doing in training. Now get off and enjoy the rest of the evening, because I want you all up early for a session before school tomorrow. We'll meet in the hall at seven in the morning.'

The boys looked around at each other – this was a serious sacrifice, but they understood that they had a great chance of some more rugby glory and were all prepared to do what was necessary.

'I don't know about the rest of you, but I won't be able to sleep tonight anyway,' chuckled Dylan as he threw his bag over his shoulder and walked out of the dressing room with his hand above his head showing four fingers.

CHAPTER 31

The Young Historian of the Year competition was held every year in the main hall of the Royal Dublin Society in Ballsbridge in Dublin. Hundreds of boys and girls from all over Ireland came to show off the projects they had worked upon all winter. Eoin was delighted when Mr Lawson told them the week before that eight of the boys – including him – had been selected to present their entries on a stand at the exhibition.

The night before it opened Eoin wandered down to the stream carrying Dave Gallaher's artefacts. And, sure enough, the spirit appeared.

'Hi, Dave, I just came down to tell you that my project was accepted for the exhibition, so it will be on show for the next three days. And will you be able to make it into Lansdowne Road for the final next week?'

'That's great news, best of luck in both of them. I'm sure I can wander down to the paddock for that. It would be nice to get a look at the ground after all those years.'

Because so many of the teachers had said nice things about the project, Eoin was nervous as the judging of the competition drew close. He decorated his little stand with photos from various stages of Dave Gallaher's life, and wrote out the 'Waste' poem in large letters on yellow card, to which he attached the document his grandad had given him. He made a little platform by covering a biscuit tin with shiny blue paper, and on top he placed the original photo of Dave's wife and daughter with the silver fern crest alongside. Across the top of the stand was printed his name and school in black letters.

He looked around the hall – lots of other students had produced amazing projects about the Black Death, Ancient Rome, Egyptian mummies and bloody battles from long ago. Eoin was sure his effort hadn't a chance against these colourful exhibits.

Dylan had also been selected for the exhibition and set up his project on the stall opposite Eoin's. The boys enjoyed talking about their work to other students, the judges and members of the public who called by. In quiet moments they discussed the upcoming game, which again pitted Castlerock against St Osgur's.

'They won't be half as easy to beat in the Aviva,' said Dylan, 'They'll be really up for the game second time round. I hope Richie keeps his trap shut this time.'

'Huh, you not hanging around with him anymore?' asked Eoin.

'Nah, I'm keeping a low profile, and he's a bit too loud for my liking,' explained Dylan.

Just then, a man asked Eoin a question about his project. As he answered him Eoin noticed that Dylan was staring at the back of the man's head with a terrified expression on his face. He turned and ran into one of the adjoining halls.

Eoin continued talking to the man, who seemed pleasant enough.

'And tell me, are you long in Castlerock yourself?' he asked.

'This is my second year there,' he answered. 'I came up from Ormondstown.'

'Well, now,' said the man, suddenly very interested. 'I only travelled up from that town this morning. A very nice place it is, too.'

'Do you live there?' asked Eoin.

'No, I was staying in the hotel on Main Street. Some members of my family live there and I was checking up on them. Do you know any other lads from Ormondstown in Castlerock?'

Eoin suddenly got a bad feeling about the man, and quickly shook his head.

'No, I'm the only one,' he said.

The man looked over Eoin's shoulder at Dylan's project on Celtic mythology. 'That looks quite interesting too. Where's the lad who wrote it?'

Eoin shrugged and said, 'I don't know, he was there a minute ago.'

The man spent a few minutes looking at Dylan's project before, looking at his watch and sighing. As he turned away, he dropped his wallet on the floor. Eoin bent to pick it up, and handed it back to the stranger.

'Do tell the boy that I thought his project was excellent,' he said. 'Although, not as good as yours, of course.'

And with that he was gone. Eoin watched as he headed for the exit, and tried to get Dylan on his mobile, but it was engaged. He kept trying, and several minutes later he got through.

'Is he gone?' asked Dylan.

'Yeah, he left the building about ten minutes ago,' said Eoin. 'Who was that?'

But Dylan had already hung up. He returned looking pale and drawn, and kept glancing all around him.

'I've been on to Mr McCaffrey and he's coming in to collect me,' he explained. 'Can you keep an eye on my project for me, Eoin?'

'Yeah, of course,' he replied. 'That man was asking all sorts of questions about school – and he said he'd just come from Ormondstown. Who is he?'

'Don't breathe a word of this to anyone Eoin, but … he's my dad,' blurted Dylan.

'Oh, no!' he added. 'It looks like he's stolen something off your stall too.'

Eoin turned quickly to see where Dylan was pointing. And there, on top of his blue platform, sat the photo Dave had given him. But the silver fern was gone.

CHAPTER 32

Eoin called up to the exhibition office to report the theft, but the organisers didn't give much hope of it turning up. Eoin realised that the stranger had dropped his wallet deliberately to distract him, and had pocketed the scrap of cloth when Eoin stooped to pick it up. He was distraught, and terrified about what Dave would say about losing the priceless badge.

Mr McCaffrey wasn't particularly interested either, when he arrived, being more concerned with getting Dylan out of the hall.

He returned an hour or two later, just in time for the award ceremony.

Eoin was still preoccupied with the theft when the chief judge stood up to announce the winners. He went on and on about the great standard of entries, and how heartening it was to see such passion for history among the students of Ireland, and … then Eoin perked up his ears. What was that he had just said?

Alan, standing beside him, dug him in the ribs. The judge continued '… a fascinating project that uses fabulous artefacts and detailed eye-witness accounts about a great rugby player who was born in Ireland and made his name as captain of the New Zealand All Blacks. This year's prize for the Young Historian of the Year goes to a boy from Castlerock College in Dublin – Eoin Madden!'

Eoin was stunned. He hadn't believed the teachers who told him how good his project was – but they had been proved right. He opened his mouth when Alan poked him again. 'Go up, Eoin, they want you on the stage.'

Eoin didn't know where to look as he stood looking down at the hundreds of people who were now staring up at him. Two television cameras were pointed straight at him and a government minister was waving a huge silver cup in his direction. He handed it to Eoin, and an envelope too, and suddenly gave Eoin the microphone. The boy stared at it for a second, and then looked up at the crowd.

'Thank you. Thank you very much,' he said. 'Thanks

to my teachers, and my grandad, and all my friends who helped me.'

Standing up on stage was a bit scary, and he really didn't know what else to say, so he handed the microphone back and waited as a dozen photographers poked and pulled him into various groupings to take pictures for what seemed like an hour.

Eventually he walked down the steps into an empty hall, and returned to his stand. He had taken the old photo with him, but the absence of Dave's All Black crest was haunting him.

'Master Madden, what wonderful news!' came a cry from twenty metres away. Mr McCaffrey and Mr Lawson rushed up to their pupil, and the headmaster offered his hand in congratulations.

'A very well-deserved victory for a brilliant project,' he gushed. 'The judges said you showed remarkable insight into what it was like to be in the trenches of Flanders. And they thought your story of how Gallaher died was truly remarkable and made it almost seem as if you were there.

'You have also won a remarkable prize for the school of a trip to any historic site in Europe. I will have a word with Mr Finn and Mr Lawson to see where we will take the boys,' the headmaster added.

'Sir, I don't want to seem cheeky,' said Eoin. 'But I'd like to suggest that we go to Ypres to see the battlefield and the cemeteries. I think the class would like that.'

Mr McCaffrey stopped, and looked at Mr Lawson. 'Well, he's the one who earned the trip,' said the history teacher. 'I suppose he should have a say in it …'

Mr McCaffrey nodded. 'Are you sure you wouldn't prefer to see Rome, or Athens, or somewhere warm and sunny like that?' he asked. 'It's just that Belgium is just … so boring.'

CHAPTER 33

For the second time in a year Eoin was the hero of Castlerock, but he was more concerned about Dylan, and about Dave's missing treasure.

Dylan had been moved out of the dormitory and was now living in the headmaster's house.

'Mrs McCaffrey's a great cook,' he told his friends between classes one day. 'She has me spoiled with the huge spreads she's giving me. Dessert every day too.'

'Careful now or you won't be in any state to be running up and down that wing,' warned Eoin. 'You're our secret weapon in the final – Osgur's have never seen you before.'

After school, Alan suggested to Eoin that they go for a run.

'What do you think is going on with Dylan?' he asked, as they jogged around the playing field. 'It's all very mysterious.'

'I can't tell you, Alan, but something happened up in the RDS and they're all a bit worried about him. I hope they allow him play in the final,' answered Eoin.

'Speaking of the RDS,' said Alan, 'did you tell that ghost that you lost his piece of cloth?'

'No, to be honest I've been putting it off for a few days. Want to head down there now to give me some support?' asked Eoin.

The boys jogged down to the woods, with a quick stop off at the dorm to collect the Gallaher family photograph. Alan and Eoin sat chatting on the rock for a few minutes before the uniformed ghost made an appearance.

'Hello, Eoin, who's your pal?' he asked.

'Hi, Dave, this is Alan, he's my room-mate in the school.'

Alan stared, open-mouthed. He had never seen a ghost before, but Eoin had talked so much about his other-worldly pals that he wasn't scared at all.

'Nice to meet you, mate – is that my photo you have there, Eoin?' asked Dave.

'It is, and it helped me to win the overall award at the contest,' he replied, going on to explain about the prize.

'That is excellent news, well done. So they're all talking about Davie Gallaher and his All Black Originals are they?'

'Yes, they were. A lot of people were very interested in the story. It even got on the televis—' Eoin stopped, realising Dave had been long dead before TV was available.

'Where's the silver fern?' asked Dave.

'Well, that's what I came here to tell you. A thief took it off the stand when I turned away for a second. The headmaster told the police, so hopefully it will turn up. I'm really very sorry. I only let them out of my sight for one second …'

Dave's face fell, and there was a brief flash of anger before he sighed.

'Oh, that's a terrible shame, but at least you didn't lose my photograph. That would have been too much to bear. Let me know if the fern turns up, won't you?'

'I will, of course,' said Eoin, 'We have that final in Lansdowne on Saturday morning, I hope you can come along.'

'I'll be there, I think. I met another spirit wandering around here who turns out to be a bit of a rugby man himself. Name of Brian. He's going to show me the way to the old ground.'

CHAPTER 34

The day of the final dawned and Dublin found itself under bright, blue skies, even if it was a little chilly. Dylan was still living in the headmaster's house, but joined the team for breakfast in the main hall.

'Right, lads, Mrs McCaffrey wouldn't let me have two breakfasts on the day of a big game so I'm slumming it a bit here today,' he joked.

'She's right! You're getting a little pot belly with all that ice cream she's feeding you,' said Rory.

'Ah now, Rory, I'd still be quicker than you with a ten-course banquet inside me,' shot back Dylan.

'All right you two, stop it there. We're all on the one team today and I don't want any squabbles,' said Eoin.

The two rivals grinned, and shook hands. 'Only messing Eoin,' laughed Dylan. 'I'm enjoying my new role as wizard on the wing. The captaincy is the only thing I have in my sights now!'

'You're welcome to it,' grinned Eoin. 'It's more trouble than it's worth sometimes.'

The boys discussed the big day ahead, and Eoin explained how his family were all coming up for the final.

'Oh dear, I should have asked,' said Dylan. 'My mum and sister are coming up too – but I think they're getting the bus. I'm sure your dad wouldn't have minded bringing them …'

'Yes, I'm sure he would have been delighted to. I'll see if I can get them a lift home anyway,' Eoin replied.

The game was a curtain-raiser for a big Leinster fixture, so kick-off was at 12.30pm. After breakfast the boys were taken by bus down to Sandymount Strand, where they strolled along the beach as part of a Castlerock tradition that dated back to the nineteenth century. From there they walked the half-mile or so to Lansdowne Road, where they were reunited with their kit-bags.

The Castlerock boys were in the same dressing room as the year before, and Mr McCaffrey told them this was an omen that they would be just as successful today.

Mr McRae wasn't quite as convinced. 'OK, guys,' he said, after the headmaster had left, 'don't bother with any of that superstitious stuff. Leave your rabbit's foot in the bag, and forget about any black cats you met today. This is all about rugby football, and you proving that you are able to put more points on the board than St Oscar's, or whatever they are called.

'Having seen you play this team twice before, I know you have better skills, and we have a good plan worked out to beat them again. But if you don't follow the plan, and back up your team-mates at every turn, then we won't get those points. So go out there and prove it to the world. You are going to bring the Begley Cup home tonight, so go out on that glorious paddock and do it – for yourselves, your friends, your families, and for Castlerock.'

The teams ran out onto the famous turf, and after a few minutes kicking and passing the ball around, the referee blew his whistle to call the captains together. Eoin had been so focused on the game that he had forgotten to look to see where his parents were sitting. There was no sign of them in the sponsor's box they had sat in last year, but he soon found them as there were no more than a few hundred spectators, and most of them were his own age or younger. He gave his family a quick wave, before resuming his duties as captain.

St Osgur's kicked off the game, and quickly showed

that they had improved the team which had been hammered in the earlier meeting in Castlerock. Their very first attack led to a try, and a powerfully-struck conversion meant they were 7-0 up before many of the supporters had taken their seats. Eoin looked at Rory as he prepared to kick off again.

'Nothing to worry about, Eoin, just work on what Mr McRae told us,' said the scrum-half.

Both sides traded penalties during the first half, but with time ticking away before the break, Castlerock won a good heel from a scrum on their opponents' 22. Rory snapped the ball back to Eoin, who spied a large gap appearing behind the St Osgur's left winger. With a delicate swing of his right boot he chipped the ball over the forwards and watched as it bobbled along the ground towards the corner flag. Suddenly, and in a glorious blur of green and white, Dylan hared along the touchline past his marker, and dived just as the ball landed on the try-line. His hands landed with a 'slap' on the white ball, and he fell face down in the soft grass.

He stood up, arms straight in the air, and waited for his team-mates to engulf him. After a few seconds, the referee broke up the delighted huddle, and directed Eoin to convert the try. As he walked back, he heard a weedy cry from the stands.

'Brilliant, Dylan, you're brilliant!' came the call, which was easy to pick up in the near-empty stadium.

Eoin grinned, and looked up to see Dylan's sister Caoimhe waving down at him. They were sitting close to Eoin's parents, but when Grandad pointed at the posts he knew he had to concentrate on the tricky kick. There was a strange wind swirling around the stadium, and Eoin was struggling to master it. He was too far out to try to spear it directly, so he just launched it in the air, trying to allow for the wind and hoping it would carry between the posts. Unfortunately, at the last second a gust tugged the ball in against the upright and it fell back to the ground as the touch judges brushed their knees with their flags.

The half-time whistle blew, 10-8 to St Osgur's.

'At least that's better than last year,' muttered Rory as they walked off. 'We were 10-0 down then, remember?'

CHAPTER 35

Mr McRae spoke quietly at half-time. He pointed out quickly where they were going wrong, but insisted that he wasn't at all worried because Castlerock had the weapons to win the battle. He took Eoin aside just before they went back out.

'Keep talking to your backs, Eoin. They need a bit of direction and have to concentrate more,' he started. 'Dylan keeps looking around into the stands – he's probably a bit overawed about playing at the national stadium, but he could miss a long kick or a pass if he's not tuned in.'

Eoin looked at the clock and realised they had a couple of minutes to spare. He decided to visit the loo, just as he had the year before. And, just as then, Brian was there when he came out.

'You're playing well, Eoin. I wouldn't be too concerned about being behind on the scoreboard. I like the look of that little winger, he's very fleet of foot. I met your pal Dave Gallaher – he's a bit sore about losing that memento, but he forgives you. Now get back on the field and let me see how much you've come on since last year.'

The second half started with a bang as second row Pearse Hickey went on a thundering charge which was only halted four metres from the line. Castlerock controlled the ball through a series of rucks before Rory flipped the ball past Eoin to where Richie was waiting. He broke inside and was tackled on the line. As he released the ball Dylan snatched it and burrowed in to touch down. Castlerock try – and the lead!

Dylan looked up to where his mum and sister had been sitting, but was surprised to see they weren't there. 'They must be late back from their half-time hot dog,' grinned Eoin, as he prepared to slot the ball over for the conversion points and a 15-10 lead.

'Has anyone ever scored a hat-trick of tries on their Lansdowne Road début?' asked Dylan, as Castlerock enjoyed a break a few minutes later as one of the St Osgur's props was treated by the physio.

'Take it easy, Dylan,' snapped Eoin. 'The only thing

that matters today is that we end the game with more points than them – it's a team game, it's not about one player's glory!'

Dylan nodded, and dropped his head, sheepishly. He walked back out to the left-wing and waited for play to resume.

With five minutes left, Castlerock held their five-point lead, but St Osgur's had been camped in their half for quite a while and were looking more and more likely to score. A trip by Eoin nearly caused disaster, as his opposite number saw the gap and almost made the breakthrough. A thumping tackle by Richie Duffy floored him, and Eoin nodded his thanks.

The St Osgur's scrum-half flipped the ball out the line, and the centre tried a long pass out to the left winger, who was standing on the touchline. With remarkable speed of thought and foot, Dylan burst into the gap and snatched the ball from the air. He tucked it under his right arm and hared off up the field as fast as his legs could carry him. The opposition's backs chased as hard as they could, but realised there was no catching the little winger.

Rory, who had spotted the move and chased off to support Dylan, was on his shoulder as he reached the try-line. Dylan looked back to see his former rival for the scrum-half spot, and slowly and gently tossed the ball back to him. Rory grinned, and touched the ball down between the posts, before turning to embrace Dylan.

The pair trotted back to the half-way line each with an arm over the other's shoulders.

Eoin patted the pair on the head in turn, giving Dylan an extra one for his selfless action. With the conversion Castlerock were now 22-10 ahead and there would be no way back for St Osgur's.

When the final whistle came, Dylan ran up to Eoin, but he didn't look at all like a player who had just won the cup for his school at the Aviva Stadium.

'Have you seen Mum and Caoimhe?' he asked. 'I haven't seen them at all during the second half. That's not like Caoimhe at all – and she's hard to miss.'

Eoin turned to see Mr McRae jogging onto the field and heading straight for them. And he was followed by Mr McCaffrey and a member of the Garda Siochána.

CHAPTER 36

'We need you to come with us now, Dylan,' said the headmaster. 'There's been an incident and we need to make sure you're safe.'

'Of course I'm safe,' said Dylan. 'I've been playing rugby for the last hour and a half, but besides a few knocks I'm fine.'

'No, son,' said the Garda. 'We need to be sure you're in a safe place for the next while. Your sister has disappeared and we're searching everywhere for her. We have reason to believe you are also a target.'

'A target!' said Dylan. 'For who?'

'We think your father has taken Caoimhe,' said the headmaster. 'He was spotted near the ground today. Your sister went to buy a drink at half-time and never came back to her seat. Your poor mother is in an awful state. Now come along with Inspector Condren here and he'll make sure no harm comes to you.'

Dylan left immediately, with the Garda keeping his hand firmly on the boy's shoulder as they walked off the pitch.

'I suppose you better go to collect the trophy now, skipper,' said Mr McRae. 'Don't mention this to the team. They'll find out soon enough and they need to enjoy the moment of victory – and congratulations by the way; that was a superb win.'

Eoin walked slowly from the field, his head reeling by what he had just heard. He knew Dylan's father was a criminal, but this seemed a terrible thing for anyone to do.

The Castlerock supporters cheered and he received dozens of claps on the back as he went up the steps to the VIP box to collect the Begley Cup. He made a very short speech which thanked everyone he needed to thank, but no more. He wanted to get back to the dressing room as soon as possible.

He collected the cup and his medal, before taking the steps down two at a time. At the bottom he handed the trophy to Mr McCaffrey and headed inside.

Passing several Gardaí on the way, he reached the dressing room just as a now-dressed Dylan was leaving. His team-mate was very upset and Inspector Condren shook his head at Eoin.

As Dylan left, Eoin placed his hand on his shoulder and whispered, 'Everything will be fine.'

The rest of the team arrived in the dressing room soon after, but their delight was soon cut short when Rory piped up.

'What was all that with Dylan at the final whistle? What was the Garda doing on the pitch?' he asked, looking at Eoin.

'I can't say,' the captain replied. 'Just enjoy the win guys – we may have been in this very same place last year with our winners' medals, but that's no guarantee that we'll ever be here again. Savour this victory, you've really earned it.'

But no one really had the stomach for any celebrations – no matter what Eoin said, they all knew something was very wrong with Dylan.

Eoin went into the bathroom once again, more to escape the questions and gloomy mood that had descended over the victors.

As he stood looking in the mirror, Brian suddenly appeared over his shoulder.

'Eoin, come quickly,' he said. 'I saw something terrible happen and you can help.'

'What, what is it?' asked Eoin.

'I was up on the middle deck at half-time,' said Brian,

'just wandering around minding my own business, I was. And just as I was heading up the steps for the second half I spotted a big, burly man grab this little girl with red hair. He came up behind her and put a handkerchief over her mouth. I knew he was up to no good, so I followed him.

'He went down in the lift and carried her out along the tunnel. It was quiet at that stage and nobody saw him. He put her into the back of a red van in the corner of the car park and came back towards the stand. I was watching him all through the second half and made sure he didn't move.

'I spotted Dave Gallaher down by the pitch and he's been helping me. He's out the back now keeping an eye on the van. He'll give me a whistle if your man comes back.'

'And where is the kidnapper now?' asked Eoin.

'He's just outside the door here,' said Brian. 'Who is he looking for?'

'He's looking for Dylan, the left winger,' explained Eoin. 'He's his father. The girl is Dyl's sister.'

'What will we do?' asked Brian.

'I'll go outside and try to find a Garda – there were plenty of them around earlier on,' Eoin said. 'Can you try to find my mate, Alan? He was able to see Dave Gallaher this week so he may be able to see you. Show him where the van is and get him to tell the Gardaí.'

Eoin went back to the dressing room and quickly pulled on his tracksuit. Throwing his kit-bag over his shoulder, he rushed out of the room and down the corridor towards the tunnel under the stands. As he reached the doorway, he found it was blocked by a familiar figure – it was the man he had met at the Young Historian Exhibition.

'Have you seen Kevin? Or "Dylan", as you call him?' he growled.

'No, he's still in the dressing room,' said Eoin, eager to get away.

'He's not. He left there ten minutes ago,' said the man.

Eoin turned, and made to go back down the corridor. The man grabbed him by the back of his collar, and pressed a handkerchief over his mouth. Eoin inhaled, and could just taste a nasty chemical when he blacked out.

CHAPTER 37

Eoin woke up soon afterwards to find he was in a dark, smelly place. He still felt groggy from the knockout drug, but he could hear the sound of someone crying close by. He opened his eyes wider, and could just make out the shape of a head. As his eyes got used to the darkness he recognised the curly hair – it was Dylan's little sister.

'Caoimhe,' he whispered, 'this is Eoin. Remember? I called to see Dyl in Ormondstown.'

'Yes, I remember.' she sniffed. 'What's going to happen? Where are we?'

'I think we're in a van in the car park of the stadium. It hasn't moved so I think we're still there. Hold tight – he's trying to find Dylan.'

But the man wasn't having any luck in the hunt for

his son. He dodged the Gardaí as he wandered the stadium, but couldn't find his son anywhere. He decided to cut his losses and head back to the van. 'At least I've got the one of them,' he muttered to himself.

On the way he debated with himself about what he was going to do about Eoin.

Meanwhile, Brian had scoured the faces of the Castlerock fans milling around the food and drink outlets after the game. Some were staying on for the Leinster match, others were keen to get back to the school to continue the celebrations. He went back out to the car park, where Castlerock's buses were idling just inside the gate. Brian looked across at the far corner where the red van was still parked.

He watched as all the pupils climbed aboard the bus, before he spotted a small boy with scruffy blond hair staring right at him. He waved at him, and called out 'Alan?'

Alan continued to stare as he walked towards him.

'Alan – I'm Brian,' he gasped.

'I think I worked that out,' said Alan, not noticing the funny looks his fellow students were giving him as he spoke, apparently, to fresh air.

'You have to come with me – Dylan's little sister is in trouble. I need your help!'

'What can I do?' he said, walking around to the back of the bus where he could avoid the curious stares of the boys who thought he was talking to himself.

'Do you see that red van over there?' Brian pointed. 'Well a kidnapper put her in the back of it.'

With that, another figure came around the side of the coach. It was Dave Gallaher.

'Brian, Alan, you need to come quick,' he told them, 'He's got Eoin now. He put him in the motor and went back inside. But he's on his way back out now.'

Dave pointed at the man as he walked down the steps and into the car park.

Thinking quickly, Alan rushed over to where two Gardaí were standing.

'Sir, are you looking for a missing girl?' he asked.

'Yes, of course,' said the officers. 'What do you know about that?'

'I think I saw that man over there carrying a girl into the back of his van,' Alan gasped.

The Gardaí looked at each other before sprinting across the enormous car park.

'Stop right there,' they called, as the man reached his vehicle.

Dylan's dad jumped inside and got it started immediately, and drove the van at speed towards the two policemen. They dived out of the way but were left floundering on the ground as the kidnapper headed for the exit.

However, Alan had filled in Mr McRae on what was happening, and the quick-witted teacher hopped into the driver's seat of the school bus. He stepped on the pedals and quickly guided the bus sideways across the exit to the car park, before telling the boys to get off the bus as quickly as they could and to run towards the West Stand.

When the kidnapper turned his car to face the exit, he saw that his way was blocked – and that he was trapped inside the car park. He sped up to the gate and jumped out of the car, but saw, to his dismay, that Mr McRae had parked the bus so tightly against the fence that he couldn't even escape on foot. His shoulders slumped, defeated, and he was quickly pounced on by several Gardaí.

Mr McRae rushed across to the red van with Alan and they opened the back doors of the kidnapper's vehicle just as Dylan walked out of the back door of the grandstand with his Garda escort. The boy stared at the scene, before quickly understanding what was going on and making for the back of the van.

Mr McRae took his penknife to the ties that bound Eoin and Caoimhe hand and foot, and the pair emerged blinking into the sunny afternoon. Dylan's mum came rushing out of the stadium, accompanied by Mr McCaffrey, just in time to see her husband being bundled into a Garda car and her son and daughter embracing joyfully.

'Did you win?' was the first question Caoimhe asked Dylan. 'After all that's happened, I really hope you did.'

CHAPTER 38

After Dylan's dad had been driven away, and the Gardaí had finished questioning Eoin and Caoimhe about their ordeal, Mr McCaffrey returned to the stadium to collect them.

'Alan Handy was quite a hero,' the headmaster said, as they sipped tea in his office in Castlerock. 'If he hadn't told the Gardaí and Mr McRae about the van, who knows what might have happened. I'm still not sure how on earth he spotted the little girl being put in the van, but all's well that ends well.'

'Well, I'm just delighted that everyone came out of it unhurt,' said Dylan's mother. 'I was truly terrified for a while there. Caoimhe and Eoin were very brave too.'

'Well, I didn't do very much,' shrugged Eoin.

'No, you were very good to Caoimhe,' replied her

mum, 'and she was much happier when you were in the van.'

'Well, I'm just glad it's all over – and we have another lovely trophy to remind us of the drama,' chuckled Mr Finn, who had just come into the office with Dixie Madden and Eoin's parents.

'Yes, but a trophy wouldn't have mattered very much if any of these fine youngsters had been hurt,' said Dixie.

Eoin smiled at his grandad.

'And I understand extra congratulations are in order,' Grandad added. 'It has been quite a week for you.'

'Yes,' Eoin blushed, 'I suppose it was.'

'Where are you going on that trip with your class?' the old man asked. 'And can I come too?' he joked.

'I'm afraid that won't be possible Mr Madden,' interrupted the headmaster. 'They only pay for twenty-two boys and three teachers. But we are going to the place Eoin requested – the battlefields of the Western Front in the Great War. I'm sure the boys will learn a lot from it and we can pay our respects to Dave Gallaher too.'

Eoin smiled, relieved that the headmaster had agreed with his suggestion. But talk of Dave Gallaher only reminded him that he had failed his ghostly friend by losing the precious piece of cloth.

Another knock came to the office door, and in walked

Inspector Condren.

'Well, Mr McCaffrey, Mrs Coonan, that all worked out well in the end. He won't be troubling you for a long time yet. He had planned to take Caoimhe and Dylan away to the continent. He even had them booked on the car ferry tonight. Lord knows what he had planned for Eoin though.'

Eoin winced, and the adults chatted about the dramatic afternoon for a few more minutes before the senior Garda rose to leave.

'Oh, I almost forgot,' he said. 'When we searched the perpetrator, we found this on him. One of the lads in the station recognised it and we worked out where he got it soon enough.' He handed a clear plastic bag to Eoin, inside of which was a ragged piece of coarse black material with the famous silver fern.

'In the end he admitted he'd stolen it from you at the RDS,' the Inspector added.

'Thank you!' gushed Eoin, overjoyed that he had recovered the precious article.

Later, once the excitement had died down and the various relatives had returned to County Tipperary, Eoin and Alan went for another ramble down to the stream.

Eoin was keen to return the crest to Dave, but there was no sign of him in his usual haunt. Brian seemed to have disappeared too.

'That was some day,' said Alan. 'I nearly got the fright of my life when I saw Brian, and I felt a right idiot talking to him in front of the whole class.'

'Fair play to you,' replied Eoin. 'You really kept your head. It must have been deadly when McRae drove the bus in front of the gates. Unfortunately I didn't have much of a view tied up in the back!'

'I didn't know what to say when the Guards asked me about Caoimhe. I told them I saw something funny and went over and heard her crying in the back. I don't think they believed me, but I couldn't tell them how I really knew.'

'No, they would have locked us up too! I don't think the Gardaí believe in ghosts,' Eoin said with a grin.

They wandered back to the dormitory block, and were delighted to see that Dylan had been returned to his place in the corner.

'Hi Dyl, that was some crack today, wasn't it?' asked Alan.

'Yeah, it was a bit scary for a while,' Dylan replied, 'but at least mum can live in peace for a while now till it's all sorted. They might even let me stay here again next year!'

CHAPTER 39

The trip to Belgium was a memorable one for Mr Lawson's history class. As head of history Mr Finn came along too, and as a special thank-you to their Kiwi coach they invited Mr McRae as well. They saw the sites of several of the battlefields, which were now mainly farmland or parks. The vast cemeteries were very moving places for the students, who listened as Mr Lawson told them the story of boys and men who came from all over the world to die in enormous numbers in this small area.

On the last day the small group drove to Nine Elms cemetery, and asked the man on the gate could he show them to the grave they wished to visit. 'Gallaher? You will not need directions,' he said. 'He is ze one with ze most visitors'.

They wandered along the rows of white gravestones, reading some names and pausing when a familiar Irish-sounding name was discovered. On Plot 11, they stopped at Row D, Number 8. The white stone had a Celtic cross carved into it, with a fern at its centre.

There was a New Zealand flag planted at the foot of the grave, and Mr Finn stooped to place an Irish tri-colour alongside. Mr Lawson told the boys about the man who lay beneath the soil, and asked Eoin to say a few words too.

'I'm never any good at this sort of thing,' Eoin started, 'but I'd like to tell you why I asked could we visit here. I thought it was interesting that a rugby legend could end up fighting in a war half way round the world from his home, but I realised they were different times to ours, and we are lucky they are. Boys only a couple of years older than us are buried here. I found the story of Dave Gallaher really interesting and wanted to come to pay respect to his spirit.'

Mr Finn asked the boys to say a quiet prayer if they wished, and then urged them back to the bus for the start of their journey home to Dublin.

'Can I have a minute on my own, sir?' asked Eoin. 'I'd like that.'

Mr Finn agreed but told him to hurry as they had to be at the airport in less than an hour.

As the teacher walked away, Eoin turned back to look

at the grave, and was only a little surprised to see Dave standing right behind the tombstone.

'This is where my mortal remains lie, but happily my spirit gets to wander the world a bit still,' he smiled.

'And I'm very grateful for that,' replied Eoin.

'I've a bit of good news too,' he added, and took the silver fern crest carefully from his pocket, still in the plastic bag.

'Ah, that's fantastic,' Dave replied, before he stopped and looked into Eoin's eyes.

'But to be honest, I didn't really miss it as much as I thought. It made me think that it's more important that pieces like this are available to the living to help remind them of the dead. You did a brilliant job on my pro-ject and I think you'd give the silver fern a good home – I'm not sure if I'll ever be back in Ireland so maybe that will help you remember me.'

Eoin's eyes started to fill up, but Dave raised his hand.

'Ah, stop that now, I'm long past tears myself and everyone that ever cared about me is long dead them-selves. Get home to Ireland and work on that sidestep. You've a cracking rugby talent and I want to hear all about you in the years to come.'

Dave placed his hand on Eoin's shoulder, and disap-peared.

Eoin walked back to the bus slowly, blinking furiously to disperse a tear.

AUTHOR'S NOTE

I first wrote about Dave Gallaher in *The Sunday Tribune* newspaper in 2001, when I bemoaned the fact that he was almost unknown in the land of his birth. A reader, Letterkenny RFC member Robbie Love, agreed. He went on to lead a campaign to rename the club's ground Dave Gallaher Park, which was crowned by a visit by several members of the All Black tourists in 2005.

References in *Rugby Warrior* to Dave Gallaher's life and death are based on real events, as is the story of the poem by Geoffrey Studdert Kennedy.

The character of Brian is based on a real rugby player, Brian Hanrahan, who died in 1927. References to his life and death are based on real events. His story is told in 'The Fatal Scrum' in *Lansdowne Road: The Stadium, The Matches, The Greatest Days* by Gerard Siggins and Malachy Clerkin (The O'Brien Press 2010).

All other references to people, alive or dead, are fictional.

'Ger Siggins, my first editor, who actually christened me RO'CK, has written [Rugby Spirit]. And it's excellent. End of.'
Ross O'Carroll-Kelly

A new school, a new sport, an old mystery ...

Eoin's has just started a new school ... and a new sport. Everyone at school is mad about rugby, but Eoin hasn't even held a rugby ball before! And why does everybody seem to know more about his own grandad than he does?